Haunted
Hearts

Lucas Mangum

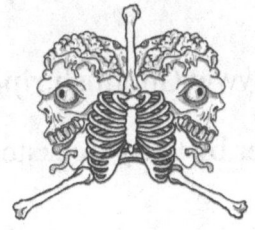

Ghoulish Books
San Antonio, Texas

Haunted Hearts
Copyright © 2024 Lucas Mangum

First Edition

www.Ghoulish.rip

Cover by Betty Rocksteady

Also by Lucas Mangum

Barn Door to Hell
Bladejob
Snow Angels
The Final Gate (with Wesley Southard)
American Garbage
Pandemonium (with Ryan Harding)
Extinction Peak
Mania
Saint Sadist
Engines of Ruin
Gods of the Dark Web

For all the ghosts who can't find rest: I give you these pages to haunt . . .

1

Abiding Glory Cemetery, September 30

We sat on the grass drinking forties while our legs dangled in front of the door to the Meier crypt. Pinprick stars dotted the near-midnight sky. The moon shone silvery through the thinning branches of a nearby elm. A cricket sang a lonely, atonal solo somewhere behind me. In one of the yards across the cemetery, a fire blazed, and I could smell the burning pine. My head buzzed with malt liquor and the hint of vanilla in Greta's perfume. She wore a green sweater and makeup that made her eyes look especially dark after nightfall. She was the only one of our trio who didn't need a nom de plume. Her last name was Graves. How fucking perfect was that? Pumpkin Ghost stood below us, shifting from foot to foot and puffing on a blunt he'd already smoked half of.

He didn't know about me and Greta, that we'd screwed a week before. The two of them were sort of a thing, but so were the three of us. Eldritch Youth. That was the name of our band, and the reason Greta and I kept quiet about our afternoon together.

That night in the cemetery, we were sort of celebrating.

It was the night before the opening of Kip Creeker's Trail of Terror.

"Where's your sister, dude?" Pumpkin Ghost asked.

"I dunno." I checked my phone. No messages. "She should've been here by now."

"Want to send her a message?" Greta asked.

I shrugged. "Kathleen's coming, too. She always takes forever getting ready."

"Well, she better hurry." Pumpkin Ghost looked at a watch that wasn't there. "Getting close to midnight."

"She'll be here," Greta said.

"Yeah."

Pumpkin Ghost took another hit off the blunt.

We just need to act like it never happened. That's all.

That's what she told me afterward when I felt a panic attack coming on. Sitting beside me now, she seemed so cool, so measured. It seemed like to her it really *had* never happened. My dad said women were good at turning themselves off. He also said they were good at hiding what they felt. He imparted both of these nuggets of wisdom in the years since his divorce from my mom. In the case of Greta, I wasn't sure which was better. If she could really switch off her emotions like my dad said women could, it was definitely better for our band, provided I could get mine under control, too. However, the fact that our tryst weighed on her, that it *meant something*, filled me with a strange excitement.

"Look, a bat!" Greta said, pointing between two trees.

We all looked up and watched it flutter in erratic directions under the moonlight. Pumpkin Ghost laughed.

"So cool," Greta said.

The little creature flew away, and we all went silent. To fill the space, I said, "That was some gas you were spitting tonight, Ghost."

He grew uncharacteristically solemn.

"Always conjuring, always exorcising."

He grinned, but it didn't have the usual brightness.

Does he know?

A car on the road separating Abiding Glory from the Trail of Terror switched off its lights and entered the cemetery gates.

"Cops?" Pumpkin Ghost snuffed the blunt.

"No, it's Jamie," I said.

Haunted Hearts

The car approached up the gravel road. Greta and I jumped down. Pumpkin Ghost followed in a slow shuffle I sometimes thought he practiced. We slid into the backseat, Greta in the middle. The dashboard clock said it was nine minutes to midnight.

Kathleen drove us to the quarry while Jamie couldn't seem to settle on a song to play on the stereo. Pumpkin Ghost typed fragments of lyrics into his phone. I tried not to think about Greta's leg resting against mine, or what it meant.

I tried not to think about what it meant the week before, her showing up at my place and asking if my mom was home, and when I said no, asking if Jamie was, and when I told Jamie was out with Kathleen, her plunging her slender fingers into my hair. What that meant. Her mouth covering mine, my lips giving way to the pressure of her tongue, the amount of time we stood making out in the doorway before I pulled away, asking why. Her calling my bluff with her hand on my crotch. What it meant, my sudden embarrassment of the unkempt bedroom she'd seen plenty of times before. As friends, I mean. How long had that crushed beer can been sitting on the desk? Did it smell weird?

Are you sure you want to do this?

What it meant, our clothes on the floor and her on top of me, rocking her hips with desperate, feral energy. Fucking me like I'd never been fucked before and like I don't think I'll ever be fucked again for as long as I live. The way she screamed when she came before switching up her rhythm, ensuring I got mine before the panic of my mom or sister coming home could kill my chances.

What it meant when she collapsed on top of me afterwards, that glint in her eyes. Our heavy breathing. How she kissed my chin and said, *Thanks, I needed that,* and how she didn't want to talk about it further, said we should probably pretend it didn't happen.

As if I could think of pretending while still inside of her.

Lucas Mangum

I believe in you, Moon Boy.

In the back of Kathleen's car with our legs still touching, I tried not to think of those perfect dimples at the base of her spine. It took everything in me to not reach for her hand or caress her knee through her black leggings.

The car stopped. Headlights beaming pale across the fence and the patch of evergreens surrounding the quarry. Three minutes to midnight.

The five of us crawled through a hole under the fence Pumpkin Ghost and I had dug when we were fifteen. Kathleen complained about getting dirty, but Jamie coaxed her through, even taking her girlfriend's hand from the other side. The trees swayed in a sudden chill breeze, and I wondered if what we came here to see had already come. I looked toward the quarry. The space above it was dark. I checked my phone.

"Shit," I said.

I showed the others. It was 12:03.

"So, what?" Jamie said. "You think ghosts really care what time it is?"

Kathleen giggled.

"It's not funny," Pumpkin Ghost said. "Certain things, well, they have meaning, you know?"

Kathleen covered her mouth but didn't stop laughing.

"Was it definitely midnight when we saw it?" I asked.

Worth a shot, I figured. It was four years ago after all. Maybe our memory was foggy.

"What, you don't remember? Man, I remember that shit like yesterday."

"It's called the witching *hour,* though, right?" Greta said. "Not the witching *three minutes*."

"Yeah, but if no one was around to see, maybe it just went back to sleep."

At this, Kathleen burst into laughter again. Jamie tried shushing her, but broke into laughter of her own.

"Let's just check it out," Greta said.

"Yeah, can't hurt," I said.

4

Haunted Hearts

Pumpkin Ghost shrugged. "Yeah, I guess, just . . . " He looked at Jamie and Kathleen. "Keep it down, okay?"

My sister and her girlfriend dummied up, but couldn't hold it in. Pumpkin Ghost marched ahead, not bothering to check if anyone else followed. Greta and I exchanged glances and went after him. I gestured for Jamie and Kathleen to come, too. A couple paces down the trail, I looked over my shoulder to make sure they had. Jamie gave me a nod. Kathleen had stopped laughing and was taking dainty, careful steps so she could avoid anything that might dirty up her outfit.

The trail was a steep decline, rocky and somewhat overgrown. The quarry had been closed down some decades ago. There were a number of different reasons given. It all depended on who you talked to what reason was the *real* reason. If you had a teacher who was interested in local history, interested enough to dedicate a whole week of classes to it, you might be led to believe a coalition of concerned parents, bolstered by environmental activists, had made a brave stand against the Landry Corporation to preserve an area of land in which kids could be kids and explore nature, a nature allowed to thrive unimpeded by the reach of industrialization. Of course, that didn't explain having a fence around the area, but such questions were discouraged. If you were bold enough to ask your teacher about the fence, you might hear that the place had, for a while, been a paradise, a Garden of Eden where wilderness and youth frolicked together, until one kid died after falling off a cliff, condemning the land. By this point, the Landry Corporation had moved on to other towns with land to exploit, so no one bothered to repeal the preservation bill, and now it just sat, barricaded off, and only explored by the more daring of our county's youth, which was, of course, all of us. It was a rite of passage.

Some of the men my dad drank with gave a different reason altogether. They said a quarry worker died in a nasty fall. This doomed, unnamed victim of an unsafe working environment happened to leave behind a rich widow who sued the shit out of the Landry Corporation, the county, the state, and maybe even God Himself. The endless litigation perpetrated by a woman no one seemed to know left the quarry fenced-in and overgrown for maybe fifteen, maybe even twenty years. One of my dad's drinking buddies claimed to have worked with the faceless dead man who launched a thousand lawsuits, even claimed to have laid the grieving widow in subsequent years, but he didn't mention any names.

Like most scenarios with multiple parties involved, all with their own special interests, I suspected some of what I heard was true, some of it was bullshit, and some of it was a little of both. Not much of it really resonated with me, truth be told. Nothing except for the third possible reason given for the closure of the quarry. This one was said to originate from Kip Creeker himself, though he didn't seem to want to talk about it whenever anyone asked him. It was the same reason the five of us headed there minutes after midnight on the first of October.

I wasn't sure *haunted* was the right word. As we approached the edge of the pit, I felt on edge myself. I so clearly remembered what Pumpkin Ghost and I saw here that night, but we were high and really *wanted* to see something. What if it never actually happened? I worried about looking stupid in front of Jamie and Kathleen, but mostly in front of Greta. Though she often claimed she believed in the possibilities of the paranormal, she remained skeptical, unlike Pumpkin Ghost who was a true believer and me who was somewhere in the middle. Greta had never been out to the quarry after midnight. She once confided in me that she'd avoided it for so long because she feared it might end up disappointing her.

We came out of the woods and reached the precipice. The vast quarry stretched before us, dark and silent. The opposite side, from what I could tell, looked a lot like our side. Shadows made it difficult to see for sure, but it was another steep drop-off, near lots of trees.

"Fucking told you guys," Pumpkin Ghost said. "These things are delicate, man."

"What exactly are we looking for?" Kathleen said.

"Doesn't matter. It's not here."

"Well, we should at least wait, right?" Greta said.

Jamie and Kathleen looked to Pumpkin Ghost for answers. He talked like someone who knew what he was talking about and that made people expect him to know things.

"I think we should," I said. "I mean, we just got here. Maybe we need to open ourselves up, relax."

"Do you have any more weed?" Greta asked.

Pumpkin Ghost shook his head. "Yeah, but back at my house."

"We have some," Jamie said. "You guys want to smoke?"

"That wasn't exactly what I had in mind," I said.

"It might not be a bad idea, though," Greta said. "It could set the mood."

"I don't know," I said. Weed had a tendency to make me panicky and weird. Being in the quarry in the middle of the night, trying to see ghosts with the friend who didn't know I'd fucked his girlfriend, I didn't need much help with that.

"Come on," Greta said. She took hold of my forearm and gave it a light squeeze. "It will be okay."

"All right," Jamie said. "I'll pack a bowl."

As if on command, Kathleen dug a baggie of the good stuff out of her purse's inside zipper compartment. According to Jamie, Kathleen got shit from her cousin in Colorado. They came in the hollowed pages of books, inside toy cars, and once, taped inside a ukulele. It was potent stuff, Jamie always testified, which worried me even more.

But Greta's hand on me steered my judgment. I

couldn't look weak in front of her. Not now. I nodded as my sister packed a bowl.

When we were all good and high, we sat on the ledge and waited.

"This is so dumb," Kathleen said, and crossed her arms. Jamie elbowed her in the ribs. "What?"

Pumpkin Ghost had a distant look in his eyes as he stared across the chasm. Perhaps he was willing the apparition to show itself. Or perhaps he was contemplating confronting Greta and me later because he suspected something. I hoped it was only the former.

Greta let her legs dangle, the only one of us brave enough to do so. I wasn't afraid of heights or anything. I just didn't like the idea of letting any part of me hang over a pit so dark and deep. Anything could be down there. Staring into the inky shadows, I could picture skeletal hands reaching up from the depths, flesh hanging off their fingers and wrists in desiccated flaps. Glowing green eyes staring back at me. Unseen, gnashing teeth fiending for teenage flesh like a smoker craves nicotine.

Greta had her hands between her knees and an expectant expression on her face. Her dark eyes staring, her auburn hair draped over her shoulders and down her back, her face flushed with intoxication. She looked so fucking cool to me then. Enigmatic. Even if Eldritch Youth never went on to do anything, I was confident she would. I supposed Pumpkin Ghost would go on to do things, too. His groupies and aspiring rappers who wanted to be him comprised healthy portions of our following. I was only unsure of myself. I didn't have fans—people hardly knew who I was. My stage presence was confined to standing behind my equipment going beep-beep-beep. It didn't matter that my work was the backbone of our compositions, an impressionistic canvas on which the others could express themselves. I needed the others for me to be fully realized; Pumpkin Ghost and Greta could each be fully realized under any circumstances, with anyone providing the space. It didn't need to be me—it only happened to be.

Greta was right: Pumpkin Ghost couldn't find out about us. We had to pretend it never happened, even though by then I'd convinced myself it meant so much.

I closed my eyes and opened them again when Kathleen screamed.

At the edge of the quarry, Kathleen was thrashing her arms and crying out. Her legs buckled like half-deflated tube men. Jamie held onto the hysterical Kathleen to prevent her from falling over the edge, but my sister appeared to be no more than a scared child herself. Pumpkin Ghost tried to conceal his laughter as this ghostly reappearance brought back bad memories which rendered me immobile. Greta stood, pulling her feet from the chasm, never taking her eyes from the rising, pale shape.

We all saw the house—I knew that right away—but Greta saw *inside* the house, just as *I* saw inside the house that night with Pumpkin Ghost four years prior. I could tell because she did the same thing I had done.

She reached out and took a step forward, then another, her foot hovering over the cliff, her torso teetering at the edge of oblivion.

I screamed and reached for her, the way Pumpkin Ghost had reached for me. I wrapped my arm around her waist and pulled her away, and then she was screaming like Kathleen, and I wondered if Kathleen had seen inside as well. I kept pulling Greta back, but she offered no surrender. She fought me with everything she had as she attempted to charge toward inevitable doom. I had to snake another arm around her and yell for Pumpkin Ghost to stop laughing and help me. He grabbed her around the shoulders, and we tackled her to the ground.

"No," she screamed. "No! We have to help her!"

Kathleen's screams became sobs. Jamie held her tighter.

Pumpkin Ghost had quit laughing and now his eyes

were wide, showing a rare fear. Greta's resistance slowed and softened.

I looked across the quarry once more.

The house was no longer there.

2

Greta's Place, October 1

When I pulled up, Pumpkin Ghost was outside smoking a bowl. Him being there wasn't part of the plan. I wanted to ask Greta about the Girl on the Borderland. She didn't tell us that night exactly what she saw, but I was fairly certain I knew. While the sight of the house awed all of us, Greta and Kathleen reacted differently. Kathleen's histrionics could've come from not preparing herself sufficiently for seeing the house, but Greta's uncharacteristic silence, her inward solemnness, suggested she'd seen something more.

Greta came out and Pumpkin Ghost shook the weed residue from his glass pipe before pocketing it in his trench coat. They sat in the back seat. After I turned out of her neighborhood, I asked, "You guys wanna talk about what we saw last night?"

They exchanged glances.

"Not really," Pumpkin Ghost said.

So, she told him. They had a secret now. I was sure they had others. This one stung especially given my recent history with Greta but also because Pumpkin Ghost used to bust my balls for how much I obsessed over the Girl on the Borderland months after he and I went to the quarry. In his defense, I had obsessed for a while. He could've been nicer, though. I guessed he had matured. Either that, or he respected her more than he respected me.

11

Not a shocker, by any means, but it still hurt whenever it became apparent.

I wondered who Greta respected more.

Who she *loved* more.

It was Pumpkin Ghost, of course.

That was why she was with him and only fucked me to—

Why *did* she fuck me?

"You guys want to talk about anything?" I asked, forcing a laugh.

Well, that was stupid. Now, he's gonna think I have something to say.

Greta glared at me in the rear view with a look that said *shut up, Moon Boy.*

Pumpkin Ghost took out his phone and started typing. New lyrics, probably.

"Hey," I said. "It's opening night! Let's get fucking crazy."

I put on *Gate of Grief* and cranked the volume. The eerie soundscapes of Kurkimilis and Malia seemed to lift the mood. We took turns humming melodies and moved to the music as I drove over slopes and took curves at fifteen over the speed limit. The trees sported leaves in various shades of purple, red, and yellow and created the illusion of a tunnel full of vibrant colors as we drove past. Greta and I shared another look in the rear view, not a glare this time, but something bright, knowing, and something like longing—maybe from her, but certainly from me. I thought about how much being with her that day felt like a culmination of so many things, some of them not even tangible, but all of them affecting me in this profound way that was too difficult to describe. It made me feel small, yet somehow meaningful.

We reached Kip Creeker's Trail of Terror, across from Abiding Glory, and I parked in front of the modest hut Kip affectionately called Creeker Headquarters. His old Econoline was already there. Sometimes, I wondered if he ever actually went home. He was either here or at whichever local watering hole had the best drink specials on a given night. The hut itself was surrounded by gray stumps and felled trees covered in moss. Kip carved a jack-o'-lantern face into one of the larger hollow stumps the year he opened. Other cars drove by on the road we'd just exited. Muscle cars with engines like chainsaws. The cool air smelled like fall. Like fallen pine needles. Like graveyard dirt. Like hard cider and nearby chimney smoke. The breeze was almost nonexistent. All these scents hung about us, unimpeded by wind. I sometimes thought I imagined such meaningful smells during the times they represented, but right now, they were all too strong and had to be real.

What happened with Greta had to be real.

The shared glance and all the weight it carried proved it beyond doubt.

Awareness of this authenticity made it all the scarier, I thought, and I tried to think of something else as we knocked on the door to Creeker's headquarters.

We waited a few seconds, then knocked again.

"Don't tell me he's late when we came here all early like a bunch of ass-kissers," Pumpkin Ghost said.

"His van's here," Greta said.

I peered into the hut's window. The place looked empty.

"Should've stayed at Greta's a little longer," Pumpkin Ghost said. "Smoked some more. Maybe drank a little."

"Ah, I hate performing fucked up."

Greta walked over to the van. She stood on her tiptoes and looked inside the driver's side window.

"He in there?" Pumpkin Ghost asked.

Greta shook her head.

"Fuck, man. Where is he?"

"Maybe he's on the trail," I said. "Fixing stuff."

"Guess we just wait here?"

"We should probably find him, let him know we're here."

"Yeah," Greta said, "if he's out on the trail, he might not have his phone with him."

"Well, you can look for him. I'm gonna smoke some more."

At this, Greta rolled her eyes. He didn't see, but I did. I nodded toward her.

"Wanna come along?"

"Sure."

I turned to leave.

"Try not to fuck my girlfriend, dude."

I stopped in my tracks. I wanted to protest, but it wasn't like he never made jokes like that before. If I protested, it would be weird and then he would know for sure something was up, so I made myself laugh and shake my head.

Several paces into the woods, Greta slipped her arm through mine.

"You okay, Moon Boy? You don't seem like yourself."

"Yeah, of course. You?"

"I don't know."

"What's going on?"

She slowed her pace and picked at her fingernails.

"I don't know. You probably don't want to hear about it."

"Then why say anything at all?"

"I don't know."

"I think you know a lot more than you're letting on."

Something shook the branches overhead. I glanced up in time to see a squirrel jump from one tree limb to another.

"Last night was something," she said. "I've never seen anything like that before."

"Did you see . . . "

Before I could finish my question, she pointed up ahead.

"Oh, no! Look!"

I followed her gesture and saw Kip Creeker, face-down in the grass.

"Shit," I said and jogged toward the fallen man.

Greta stayed close behind.

"Should I call 9-1-1?"

"I don't know. Maybe let's make sure he's not just passed out drunk or something."

We entered the clearing. I knelt beside Kip and grabbed his shoulder.

"He's not breathing," I said.

"Shit." Greta took out her phone.

I rolled Kip over. A twisted mask of agony stared up at me. One eye bulged, at least double the size of the other. Mouth frozen in mid-scream. A large gash shone angry and red on one cheek. Another cut a crimson crescent across his throat.

Then, the dead man laughed.

"Goddamn it, Kip," Greta said, pocketing her phone.

"Oh, come on, it's the season for this kinda shit," he said, sitting up and still chuckling. "If I can't fake my own death in October, when else?"

"The way you drink," I said, "we never know you're faking."

He stood. "All right, all right. We'll save these antics for our guests. Opening night, yeah?"

Greta and I loosened a little, all nods and smiles.

Kip glanced around. "Where's the rock star?"

"Back by my car," I said.

"Smoking up, I bet. He should know my policy by now." He paused for what would've been dramatic effect if we didn't know what he'd say next. "No getting high unless you brought enough to share."

The proprietor and namesake of the haunted attraction used to work in Hollywood, but a reputation for partying hard enough to become a fixture in the tabloids got him blacklisted and sent back to the rural back roads and depreciating colonials of Eastern Pennsylvania. Lucky for him, his parents left him the funeral home they ran, its neighboring cemetery, and the surrounding, wooded acres.

Having no aptitude or interest when it came to the practice of preserving corpses or dealing with grieving loved ones, he closed the funeral home and opened Kip Creeker's Trail of Terror.

When the three of us came back to the hut, Pumpkin Ghost had finished smoking and was back to typing on his phone. A couple of other employees had shown up as well: a demure redhead named Carmela who had been on last year, and Damiana, a trans woman and proud member of the local Satanic Temple, who had introduced herself a couple of weeks back in the Trail of Terror Facebook group. They rode in together and I wondered if they were dating, the way they stood close together, though not quite holding hands.

With five of us there now, Kip set to work assigning tasks. He sent Carmela down to the A/V tent so she could DJ and set up the projector to play clips from public domain horror movies on a large screen which loomed over the trail. Greta, Pumpkin Ghost, and I got dressed up and went to our respective designated areas. Pumpkin Ghost dressed in the robes of a cult leader and got the machines running inside the defunct funeral home. Greta went to the cemetery gates, dressed as a blood-spattered bride, ready to greet anyone brave enough to enter. I wore a burlap sack over my face like that killer from *The Town That Dreaded Sundown*. My job was to make sure all the attractions on the hayride route were intact and ready to go. I swept dead leaves from the makeshift gallows, turned on the timed ghost lights in the ramshackle cabin, swept deer shit from the zombie crosswalk, rehung rubber bats and spiders from the tunnel of terror's ceiling, and more or less tried to get into character. I'd get to chase a would-be victim down a route chosen in advance so anyone on the hayride could watch us run.

As the new girl, Damiana helped Kip hitch the hay trailer to his tractor. It was hard work and Kip always made a new employee do it. Despite the strenuousness of the task, getting it assigned to you actually meant Kip liked you. Carmela must have tipped her off about this because she seemed to carry out the job without complaint. The only thing she objected to was dressing up like Norman Bates in drag. She said it was transphobic to assign the role specifically to her, and after some thought, Kip agreed, apologized, and let her dress as a werewolf. Kip was an old dude, set in his ways on a lot of things, but weirdly empathetic on contemporary social issues for a guy of his generation. I suspected it might have been the Hollywood influence, but I couldn't be completely sure.

By the time only fiery streaks in the western sky remained from the passing day, darkwave throbbed through the speakers hidden in branches high over the trail where a line of attendees buzzed with anticipation. In the woods, I lay in wait with my acting victim—a woman named Latoya who I had gone to elementary school with but hadn't seen since—and clutching my prop knife to my chest like a good luck charm.

"Remember when you and the others used to call me La Toilet?" Latoya asked.

I tried *not* to remember, but of course I did. I remembered all my embarrassing, less than empathetic moments. Things done solely to get a reaction. Things done to transfer negative attention onto someone else. Things done for purely selfish reasons.

I swallowed a lump of shame. "What? No. Are you sure it was me?"

"Positive." She cocked her head to the side and gave me a look that said she wasn't buying the selective amnesia bit. Nor should she, I thought.

"Well, shit. I'm sorry."

"It's cool. Now." Her eyes gleamed with something I couldn't quite read.

Our exchange got me thinking about growing up again. Kids could be real jerks. I guessed I was no different back then. I didn't know if I was any better now, but I knew I

17

wanted to be. Since Latoya had accepted my apology, I figured now was as good a time as any to move forward. Blank slate.

"What are you up to now?" I asked, ignoring the inner voice that asked *what about Great?*.

"Nursing school."

"Ah," I said. "Actual career prospects."

"What? You don't have any aspirations?"

"Beyond the music thing, not really."

"Oh, that's right," she said. "Eldritch Youth."

"Yeah, Eldritch Youth."

For some reason, heat bloomed in my cheeks. I shifted and flexed my hand on the knife.

"Pumpkin Ghost can spit for a white dude," she said.

"Seems to be the consensus. What do you think of the beats?"

"Pretty good. You make them?"

"Yeah, I did. I mean, I do."

She smiled. "Cool."

I wondered if she meant it. Sometimes, it seemed like kids our age who went on to pursue *real* jobs thought what we did was kinda silly. Latoya was hard to read for some reason. Cute, though, and intelligent. I felt weird thinking so, like I was betraying Greta somehow, even though that was absurd.

Kip announced to his hayride passengers that they were about to enter Dire Woods, home to werewolves and a killer who just can't seem to die. That was our cue.

"Ready?" I asked.

"Let's do this," she said.

I let her get a head start of about seven paces before giving chase, stalking forward like Michael Myers himself and letting the deep throbs and harsh synths conjure the long-dormant spirits of the season.

I tried not to wonder if the house would rise tonight at midnight, even with no one watching.

I tried not to wonder if the Girl on the Borderland would come to its window and not be seen.

Haunted Hearts

I couldn't figure out why I didn't see her that night, despite seeing her the first time I went out there. Of course, a lot can change in four years, but I didn't feel like I had changed all that much. Had I? I still lived with my mom in the same house in the same town. I still composed music no one seemed to care about. Still had the same friends. Been through a few girlfriends, I guess. One of them was pretty serious.

Her name was Vivian. I didn't talk to her anymore, but I found my thoughts drifting to her as I chased Latoya through the woods. You could say she was my first love. For better or worse, she taught me everything I knew about women. On one hand, she taught me to believe in myself. She made me feel like I was attractive and talented. I lost my virginity to her and learned sex was best when taken slow, although the frantic way Greta made love to me certainly made me question this notion. On the other hand, her instability reinforced some of my father's dubious advice about women. One time we ran into a girl from school at Choctaw Lanes. It was someone I barely knew— Amanda something. Well, she gave me a hug and I guess she held onto me a little too long for Vivian's liking. Vivian shut down, giving me only one word answers all night.

When we got into the parking lot, she pulled a knife on me.

"What the fuck?" I said.

"That wasn't cool," she said. "Don't let it happen again."

I didn't even know what she was talking about. I knew something was off but had no idea she was mad enough to pull a fucking knife on me. That was some psycho shit. She'd hidden that rage until she got somewhere she could accost me without drawing attention. Like my dad warned women could do, she hid her emotions and expertly calculated when to release them. I was shocked and scared and I should've broken up with her.

Instead, I apologized profusely, and we fucked in her

19

car that night. Even in her possessive rage, she wanted to take it slow. There was something cold and clinical about the way she rode me. She put that knife to my throat each time she could feel me reaching the edge and told me I only got to get off when she said I could. When my orgasm finally came, it was devastating.

But her leaving hurt far worse.

It didn't happen right away. We stayed together another three months. I was damn careful how I acted around other women. Even Greta got hugs that were brief and stiff. She'd called me out about it later, after Vivian was gone and I'd started coming around more. I didn't know how to explain it and I said so. She gave me a gentle slug on the arm and told me we were cool. The breakup with Vivian didn't go down with as much drama as you might expect, going off of the bowling alley parking lot knife incident.

One day, she just disappeared. Deactivated all her social media accounts. Disconnected her number. Her car was gone. Not even her parents knew where she went.

Searching for Vivian in the subsequent months after our breakup was a lot like stalking through the darkness with a corn sack over my head. Probably why I was thinking of her now.

I was lost back then, searching for a woman who was essentially my abuser.

Maybe I was lost now, searching for meaning in what should have just amounted to a fun afternoon with a friend.

Searching for deeper answers beyond basic biology. *I'm hot, you're hot, let's bone.*

Did Greta think I was hot?

She at least thought I was fuckable. That was something. Maybe.

I raised my knife and stalked Latoya onto the gallows platform. She faced me, wide-eyed with her lips trembling, and sidestepped a hanging scarecrow. I shoved its straw body aside for dramatic effect. It fell, headless from its noose, and hit the weathered planks with a dull thud. The hayride passengers looked on, some laughing and some gasping. Kip was yelling something over the speaker, advertising my character as more vicious than Voorhees and more maniacal than Myers. He never called me the same name twice. One night, when particularly inebriated, he called me the Terrible Terror of the Terrible Trail of Terrible Terror. Tonight, he called Junior for some obscure reason. I guess I didn't mind. He was like a father figure in some ways. Something inspired me to do well so he would do well and think highly of me. I didn't feel that way about my other bosses. I felt that way about my real father less and less the older I got.

So, I stalked across the gallows platform like a champ, raising my knife like I had every intention of plunging it into Latoya's heart. She backed away from me, staring and whimpering and doing a pretty good job at the whole scream queen thing. I guessed she was a big horror fan.

She was supposed to turn and jump down, but she kept backing up toward the edge of the platform. I wanted to yell a warning her way, but I also couldn't break character. I winced, knowing damn well what was coming. By the time Kip caught on, it was too late. He called out to her just as her right foot went over the edge, followed by the rest of her. I heard a loud crack I hoped wasn't bone.

3

On the Road, Later

Latoya was sprawled across my back seat, ankle elevated on my backpack and a few folded sweaters. I was taking her to the hospital. I kept telling her how sorry I was.

"No," she said, "I should've been paying attention. Guess I was too caught up in trying to be convincing."

"Me too," I said.

She winced and adjusted her posture.

"You should put on your music," she said. I resumed *Gate of Grief*. After a few measures, she shook her head. "No, *your* music."

I chuckled nervously. "Oh."

I shuffled to our debut mixtape, *Wet Dreams in the Witch House*. The opening track began with a chord progression I programmed using a virtual instrument that emulated a church organ. I'd thrown guitar distortion on it to make it sound dirtier, more sinister. Greta's bass line came in with a closed hi-hat playing sixteenths, Pumpkin Ghost's cue to spit rhymes about night visits from succubi and talking rats.

"Your boy's got quite an imagination," she said.

"He reads a lot," I said, not sure if I was complimenting my friend or suggesting a lack of originality.

"Nothing wrong with that. Do you like to read?"

"Yeah, mostly comics, though."

"I thought you might be the comic book type."

I laughed, this time less nervously.

"What's that supposed to mean?"

"That you're a geek like me," she said, smiling in the rear view.

"Yeah? What books do you like?"

"Oh, God. *Anything* Brian Michael Bendis touches is pretty much brilliant."

"Oh, fuck yeah. *Ultimate Spider-Man* is fucking fantastic."

"I like his run on *Jessica Jones*."

"Like you said, everything he touches: brilliant."

I felt warm all of a sudden. Euphoric.

We reached Saint Theresa's and I helped Latoya out of the car. Inside, the receptionist, a gray-haired woman with a mouth pinched in a perpetual scowl, asked for Latoya's insurance card.

"I don't have one." The receptionist's frown deepened. She looked Latoya up and down. "I'm insured, though."

Latoya handed over her license and the receptionist called the insurance company, never loosening her frown.

"What a bitch," I said, when we sat down in the waiting room.

Latoya shrugged. "Just an old racist."

"You seem so . . . . okay with it."

"Just used to it, I guess."

"Sounds like kinda a drag."

"It is, but what am I gonna do?"

She gave me a wry smile, then she squeezed my hand. I tensed. She took her hand away.

"I'm sorry," she said.

I shook my head quickly. "Don't be. I just wasn't expecting that."

"I guess I'm the touchy-feely type."

"No, it's okay." Then I took her hand. "Really."

We took a long look at each other, then got back to talking nerdy stuff. I found out she did indeed like horror. Mostly stuff like *The Walking Dead* and the *Saw* franchise.

She didn't know any of the trashier stuff Greta and I enjoyed. That was okay. They could just be for Greta and me. This, with Latoya, was something else, not better or worse, just *different*, and maybe—probably—not romantic at all.

When they called her name, I helped her to her feet. She gave me a hug and thanked me for taking care of her.

"Will you need a ride home?"

"No. My mom will be here."

"Okay, cool."

"See you around," she said, as the nurse helped her into a wheelchair.

I left the hospital, not sure how to feel about everything.

I drove back to Creeker Headquarters to check in with everybody. I wanted to see that Greta and Pumpkin Ghost got home okay. Plus, I wanted to make sure Kip wasn't too depressed about how opening night played out. He was the only one left when I returned. A bottle of Old Crow sat on his desk. He hadn't bothered getting a cup. He offered me the bottle. I waved it away.

"No, I'm good."

"Want a beer?"

I went to the mini-fridge beside his desk and pulled out a Yuengling Lager.

"Sorry tonight didn't go smoothly."

"Not your fault, kid."

"I feel like it sorta is."

"Ah, accidents."

"You have anyone who can step in and play my hapless victim tomorrow night?"

He shook his head. "You know anyone?"

"I could ask my sister, Jamie."

She'd worked at the Trail of Terror the previous year. It wasn't really her scene. She said we were too cliquish, but I bet she'd help if I asked her.

"How's she been?"

Haunted Hearts

"Good. Dating someone, I think."

"They grow up fast," Kip said, and took a pull from the whiskey.

I couldn't remember if he had kids or not.

"You know I used to make movies?"

I knew, and he should've known I knew, but I got the impression he had something else to tell me, so I nodded.

I waited for him to say more, but he just stared at the calendar on the wall. It was turned to October. OPENING NIGHT was written in red Sharpie on October 1. Regardless of the weekday it fell on, he always tried to open October 1st, even if the rest of the month he only stayed open Thursday through Monday. He said it was special, and I guessed it was special to me, too. It was the beginning of the time everyone else cared about all the spooky shit I loved all year long. I watched Kip pick the red marker off his desk and cross out the date. He stared some more, not saying a word. I wondered if I should say something, but I could only watch him and wonder what he was thinking.

He blinked as if waking from a trance and turned to me. He nodded toward the bottle in my hand.

"You gonna drink that?"

"Probably not. You want it?"

"You can just put it back."

I replaced it in the mini-fridge.

"See you Thursday?" I asked.

"Yeah, see you Thursday. And don't forget to ask your sister."

"I won't."

I drove home with my trap mix playing on shuffle. On the wooded back roads, it was like driving through the void on some surreal highway. On either side, the blackness was impenetrable.

My thoughts looped. Was Kip going to be okay? Did Greta see the Girl on the Borderland? Did Pumpkin Ghost know about us? Would something happen with Latoya and me? I even wondered what might have happened to Vivian.

25

Lucas Mangum

My thoughts were celestial bodies circling a star which held my future. I had to pass through each of their orbits to see it fully illuminated.

When I got home, my house was dark. Jamie was either asleep or out with Kathleen. I would have to ask her about filling in for Latoya in the morning. Hopefully, she would say yes. I got out of my car and walked the wooded path up to my front porch. We didn't have any lights around the path, so I had to go entirely by memory. The night sky seemed darker than usual, the moon and stars obscured by the overcast sky. The small creatures of the night created a wall of sound around me, as impenetrable and impressive as the darkness itself. Though nineteen, I climbed the path at a brisk pace and didn't look back. Maybe it was the somewhat isolated location, or maybe it was the twists and turns the night had taken while spending time around all that horror iconography, but I got it in my head that I needed to get inside quickly. Something childish and primal propelled me. I kept my gaze locked onto the lone outside light, which hung over the corner of the front door. It was cocooned by the web of a spider clever enough to know that the light would bring moths and flies for it to trap and feed upon.

I reached the patio at the end of the path and separated my house key from the others on the ring. A twig snapped somewhere nearby. Too nearby.

I froze in my footsteps, my shoulders pinching my neck, my chest going tight. I slotted the key between the knuckles of my right hand's two forefingers. Listened for footsteps. For heavy breathing. The air was still; my ragged breath and the pulse of the night insects were the only sounds.

I tried to relax my shoulders and took a step toward the door.

Someone covered my eyes from behind.

"Guess who," a familiar voice said.

I twisted and ducked out of the interlaced hands

26

covering my face. I turned, needing to see her to know she was there, that I hadn't completely lost my shit. Then I saw Vivian standing on my patio, and any self-control I had left eroded like pollen on a windshield in the rain.

"What the fuck? Seriously, what the fuck?"

"Keep it down," she said, her voice all easygoing like she hadn't just shown up to my house uninvited after dropping off the face of the earth for almost a year.

"Don't tell me to keep it down. What are you doing here? Where have you been?"

"Just relax, Mooney. It's fine."

"No. And I hate that fucking name."

"Okay-okay. Just . . . you're gonna wake your mom and make it weird."

"As if it isn't already."

She gestured to the bench that stood against the side of my house. "Can we just sit and talk about it?"

I glared at her for several seconds. The glow from the light above my door gave her skin an otherworldly pallor, and the term "corpse-light," which I'd read in an H.P. Lovecraft story, drifted up from the inkier, less-charted regions of my brain. With a sigh, I said, "Okay, fine," and stepped aside for her to take a seat on the bench. I plopped down beside her and gazed into the thicket in front of me, waiting for Vivian to say something. "So, where have you been?" I asked, when she didn't speak.

Vivian hummed and lit a cigarette.

So, she was a smoker now.

"Aren't you going to ask me why I came back?"

"Sure," I said, trying to sound less shaken than I felt.

"I missed you." I looked away from her. She put her hand on my knee. "What? Didn't you miss me?"

"I don't know what to say. You just up and disappeared. Even your parents didn't know where you were."

"I told them not to tell you."

I cringed away from her. Heat flared in my cheeks. My

heart thundered so hard I worried I might end up in that rare percentage of young adults to die from a heart attack.

"Why?" I asked, this time doing nothing to hide my emotions.

She used the cherry of her first cigarette to light a second one. She took a deep drag and exhaled a plume of smoke so thick it looked almost like fog.

"Because someone was after me."

With those five words, my reality shattered. Guilt clouded my anger. How could I so selfishly think her disappearance had something to do with me? Don't get me wrong: despite regretting my anger, I wasn't sure I liked having her around again. She had, after all, threatened me with a knife. That kinda shit doesn't go away. Still, I couldn't help but feel an overwhelming urge to protect her, even after all she put me through. I couldn't explain why and didn't think I would ever be capable of doing so.

"Who?"

"It doesn't matter. You don't know them."

"It does matter."

"It's someone I knew a long time ago. That's all. They found me and I had to lay low for a while. That's it, really."

It dawned on me how little I actually knew about her. We dated for six months, and I felt like she knew everything about me. I knew she went to alternative school. I knew she was highly intelligent. She was my first, but I wasn't hers. She journaled almost religiously. She once showed me a shelf full of Moleskines. She swore she had written on every page but didn't let me see. Her birthday was October 19 and she used to go camping as a little girl. Beyond that, she remained a mystery. Now, she mentioned a stalker from her past? I couldn't believe she never brought this up before.

"They're dangerous?" I asked.

"Anybody can be dangerous under the right circumstances."

I thought again about her knife at my throat.

"Yeah."

She snuffed out her cigarette in the ashtray on my porch, which had not been used since my grandfather died.

"Can I stay here tonight?"

"What about your parents?"

"I can't wake them up at this hour. You don't want me to stay with you?"

She put her hand back on my knee.

"It might not be a great idea."

She cocked an eyebrow. "When has *that* ever stopped you?"

"You have a point there."

"So, let me stay. I'll be gone in the morning. I'm not asking to be your girlfriend again. I just need a bed. One night."

"One night."

"That's all."

"All right. Just let me go in first and make sure everyone's asleep. You mind coming in my window?"

"Sounds kind of exciting."

"It's not going to be *that* kind of visit," I said, knowing damn well how easily she could change my mind.

"Whatever you say."

When I went inside, I considered locking her out. Over and over, I told myself letting her stay was a bad idea, but I opened my window, pulled her inside, and let her pull me into bed.

4

Home, October 2

I woke the morning after opening night blissfully unaware of all that transpired while I slept. Even my own actions remained a mystery to me for those first few seconds before Vivian rolled over and draped her arm across my chest. I shut my eyes and desperately hoped it would be Greta instead, but I knew better. I turned toward her. She was already awake, her cheeks aglow, her blue eyes glinting. Our actions from the previous night all flooded back to me and I tried not to panic. I embraced her.

"That was fun," I said.

I wasn't lying. It *was* fun. Vivian knew just where to touch me, and how to respond when I touched her. Her flesh was familiar and felt like home, however haunted our house. I nuzzled up to her and we made love again.

Love. That was what this was, I grudgingly admitted.

I hated how good it felt, but also felt a sense of relief. That *coming home* feeling she inspired. This was a terrible idea, and I didn't care.

We got dressed and went downstairs. My mother was sitting on the sofa, frowning at her phone in her lap.

"Hi, Mom," I said. "You okay?"

"Good morning . . . oh, hi, Vivian. Nice to see you."

"Nice to see you, too," Vivian said.

"You're . . . you're back in town?"

"For now."

My guts clenched.

Haunted Hearts

What does that mean?

Not wanting to confront her about that in front of Mom, I frantically searched my thoughts for something I could mention to change the subject. I remembered my promise to Kip the previous night.

"Have you seen Jamie?"

"No, I was going to ask you the same thing. She . . . isn't answering my messages."

"That's not too abnormal, is it?" Vivian asked.

"She usually lets me know if she's sleeping out." Mom shook her head. "Not usually. Always."

"She's at that age, though," Vivian said, despite only being much two years older than Jamie herself. "She's a sophomore now, right?"

"If you hear from her, can you let me know?" Mom asked me, ignoring Vivian.

"Yeah, definitely. You do the same."

"Where are you two off to?"

"I was just gonna take her home," I said.

"We may stop at the West or something first, though," Vivian said.

"We will?"

"Aren't you starved? We got quite a workout last night."

Every inch of my skin got hot.

Did she really just say that shit in front of my mom?

But my mom's head was somewhere else.

"Okay," she said. "Please let me know if you hear from Jamie."

"I will."

We went out to my car. I started the engine and backed out of my driveway.

"I dunno about the diner," I said. "Trying to save my money, you know?"

"So you can liberate yourself from your mother's oppressive regime?"

"No, she's fine. It's just . . . time."

"Yeah . . . I was only fifteen the first time I moved out," she said.

She never mentioned this before, and I wondered if it was true. It wasn't unbelievable or anything, but in the sunlight and after the interaction with Mom, I found myself searching for reasons to drop her off and tell her I never wanted to see her again. New reasons, I mean.

Her flesh is familiar.

Feels like coming home.

No matter how haunted.

We were out of the neighborhood when I brought it up. "For now," I said.

"What?"

"You said you were back *for now*. What did you mean by that?"

She just smiled and shrugged one shoulder.

"I can buy us brunch," she said. "You were kind enough to let me stay with you."

"Are you sure?"

"I wouldn't suggest it if I wasn't."

"All right, well, just be glad refills on coffee are free. Otherwise, I'd run up quite a tab."

"You're such a dork," she said, and gently slugged me.

At the West, we sat at our old favorite booth, the one in the south corner. Black coffee steamed in the mug she held. I had paled mine with half and half. *Ruined it*, she used to tell me. She didn't make a comment this time.

"So, what do you think is up with Jamie?" she asked.

Her concern for Jamie struck me as odd. I wondered if it was genuine. I saw no reason it couldn't be, but then again, she was pretty dismissive about it with my mother. I could never figure her out. Back when we were together, she and Jamie got along okay but weren't exactly close. We never went out just the three of us, and whenever Vivian came over, she and I usually went straight to my room to put on a movie, have sex, or both. On the occasions we all went to dinner with my mom, though, they mostly engaged with each other, talking about music or school or the girls Jamie was dating.

"I don't know," I said. "Do you think she's okay?"

She lifted a shoulder. "Probably."

"It sucks she's not around. I had to ask her something."

"Oh?"

I told Vivian about Latoya, leaving out details such as driving her to the hospital and thinking I might be into her.

"I was gonna ask Jamie to fill in."

"I can do it!"

"I dunno . . ."

"Come on. What do I have to do? Run from you and scream a little?"

"I mean, yeah, that's basically it."

"So, what's the problem?"

"Nothing, I guess."

"So, let me fill in."

"Well, all right. Besides, by the time Jamie gets back, I'm sure it would be too short of notice for her. If she gets back. Fuck. Maybe we should call the cops or something."

"I'd make a better final girl, anyway."

I flicked at the stir straw resting against the inside of my mug. Was she even fucking listening to me?

"What else is on your mind, Mooney?"

I cringed inside at the pet name. She started calling me that when I told her I planned to use Moon Boy as my stage name. She seemed to get a kick out of doing it, so I rarely told her it bothered me.

"A lot, to be honest."

A waiter with thick glasses and a half-tucked-in black polo shirt took our order and left.

"Jamie will be fine," she said, taking my hand across the table.

"It's not just that. It's . . ."

"What?"

I didn't know where to begin. Shit, she was part of the problem. Vivian's presence almost made me forget about my concern for Greta and whatever she saw the other night at the quarry. I remembered Kathleen screaming while Jamie held her. The ghost house levitating between the eroded edges like an ethereal spaceship, aglow with sickish pale light. Greta nearly stepping over the edge to join the Girl on the Borderland in some liminal nonlife.

What if Jamie returned to the quarry?

It would be so like her to take Kathleen back there to show there was nothing to be afraid of.

"When we're done here, I need to drop you off at your parents' house," I said. "No more stalling, okay?"

"Why?" she asked, with a smirk.

I considered just telling her I had stuff to do, but the truth came out instead.

"I'm going to look for Jamie."

"Okay. And?"

"I think I know where she might have gone. I hope I'm wrong, though."

"So? Let me come. Might not hurt to have another set of eyes. Why are you so afraid of me, Mooney?"

"Don't call me that, okay?"

"Okay, okay." She made an angry cat growl.

"Sorry, it's just . . . I guess it still kind of hurts. You going away and all."

"I told you why I left."

"I just wish you would've told me then."

"Well, now you know."

"Still, that name . . . "

"Fine," she said, stretching the word out to show annoyance I couldn't decipher as real or put on. "At least let me help look for Jamie? Can you even come up with a reason why I shouldn't?"

"No, I guess not."

"See." She gave my hand another squeeze. "I'll be a good Watson. I promise."

"All right. Okay."

"Excellent," she said. "Where are we going?"

I told her.

"Ooh, Girl on the Borderland territory."

I wondered then if Vivian had seen the girl, or even the house. We never talked about it. Frankly, I was surprised to hear her mention it.

"Yeah," I said. "Yeah, I guess."

Our food came and our waiter told us to enjoy our meal.

"I know I will," she said, splitting her gaze between me and her breakfast T-bone.

Just like that, she'd managed to insert herself into three big areas of my life.

I wondered how long it would be before she once again became my whole world.

5

The Quarry, Later

"**Oh, fuck**," I said, spotting Kathleen's car parked outside the quarry fence.

I got out and trotted toward the hole we had all crawled through the other night.

Vivian lingered back at Jamie's car, looking inside for signs of life.

"Anything?" I asked.

She shook her head grimly.

I crouched by the hole and Vivian came to my side.

"We going through?" she asked.

"Yep."

"I'm proud of you, Mooney. Didn't peg you for the take-charge type."

This time I didn't reprimand her for the pet name. I simply gave her a curt nod before crawling under the fence. I stood and dusted myself off as she came through after me.

"Got your knife?" I asked.

"Yeah. Think I'll need it?"

"Dunno. I hope not."

We went up the trail, through the woods. I tried to make out any distinctive footprints, but all the impressions blended together in the loose dirt. It was impossible to tell which steps were fresh or which ones belonged to who. I didn't even recognize my own.

We came out of the woods and inched toward the pit. I steeled myself with a deep breath before looking over the precipice. In the split seconds it took for my gaze to cross the cliff's edge, I imagined seeing Jamie down there, splayed among the rocks in ruined pieces.

But the rocks below were just rocks.

"Maybe call her again," Vivian said.

"Yeah, maybe."

I dug out my phone and dialed Jamie's number. I'd already tried her a few times—once in the West's parking lot before heading out here, a couple times on the way—and I felt insane trying again and expecting a different result, but I couldn't help myself; panic had fully set in. But this time, an electronic jingle played somewhere in the nearby woods as the line rang atonally in my ear.

I ran in the direction of the ringtone, phone still pressed to my ear. I stepped over brambles and ducked under branches. Vivian followed, wincing as something caught on her clothes. I glanced back at her, but barely saw her free her shirt from a thorny vine. The sound of Jamie's phone grew louder. We were getting close, but Jamie herself was nowhere in sight. Neither was Kathleen.

I found the phone in a pile of dead leaves, screen dotted with flecks of dirt. The wallpaper image of Jamie and Mom at the pool last summer.

"Shit."

Everything in my chest tightened and I forgot how to breathe. Vivian put a hand on my shoulder, and I flinched. For a horrible moment, I forgot she was there. Thought someone else had found me. The same someone responsible for my sister going missing. Because that's what she was—missing. Finding this phone here, I no longer had any doubt.

"We're going to find her," Vivian said, with a rare tinge of sympathy in her voice.

Finding her was no longer in question. Finding her *alive* was another matter entirely. I remembered the old true crime shows Dad used to watch. The ones where young women all wound up in shallow graves, their families left with nothing but headstones and never-draining wells of grief.

Vivian squeezed my shoulder.

"Do you want to keep going?" she asked. "We can call the police if you want, if you're afraid of what we'll find."

I found myself once again in awe of her capacity for reading my mind and reminded of her occasional compassion, her uncanny abilities to sense what I needed and then provide it. No wonder she haunted me so. Could Greta be good for me in the same way if she and I were together?

I closed my eyes and made myself breathe.

"Let's keep going," I said. "If she's . . . if there's something wrong, it's better if I find her."

"Are you sure?"

"Yeah."

We trudged on through the woods, calling out for both Jamie and Kathleen. It was barely past noon, but even in the daylight, the woods were no easier navigate than if they'd been plunged in darkness.

When we reached the train tracks and spotted the cornfield on the other side, I felt truly lost. Overwhelmed, really. Maybe I should have called the police. Maybe this search was too big a job for Vivian and me. Of course it was. These woods covered several miles. Then there was the cornfield. Then there were other places where she and Kathleen could have plunged into the quarry. My legs gelatinized from the stress of facing something like this.

"It's okay," Vivian said, putting her arm around me once more.

Something moved in the cornfield. Vivian and I tightened our hold on each other and took a collective step back. It sounded larger than an animal.

"Where's your knife?" I asked.

"Maybe we should just go," she said.

But we stayed put, only moving to take alternating breaths.

Haunted Hearts

The cornstalks parted to reveal a human shape covered head to toe with dirt. They wore rags and their hair was in tangles. Blood had hardened in various places on their skin. It took me several seconds to even recognize her.

"Kathleen?"

She didn't respond. Eyes wide, lips trembling.

"Are you okay?"

"Of course she's not okay."

Vivian pulled some wet wipes from her purse and approached the terrified and probably catatonic Kathleen.

"Where's Jamie?"

"I don't think she can talk."

"Jamie!" I hollered, pushing my way into the corn. I spun around, started pacing. "Jamie!"

Vivian wiped the dirt from Kathleen's cheeks as I searched the nearby grounds, parting the stalks of corn and scanning the area, at first full of a frantic and desperate hope, which quickly turned into dismay. Finding nothing, I rejoined Vivian, and we led Kathleen across the tracks and back through the woods. In my car, Vivian rode with Kathleen in the back seat while I drove us to Saint Theresa's, the whole time wondering where my sister could be.

The emergency room at Saint Theresa's was this bizarre dream world of white walls and white floors reflecting bright fluorescents. Artificial purgatory. None of it felt real and all of it felt scary.

Someone had called the cops. Did I? I know I called my mom and listened to her voice tremble the way it did when she was trying not to completely fall apart. I told her an officer would be coming by to take a statement from her.

The police followed the orderlies wheeling Kathleen down the hall and they split me and Vivian to get answers about nothing. The cop questioning me gave me his number and I texted him a picture of Jamie and he said he didn't want to make empty promises, so there was nothing more to say after that.

All my thoughts were on Jamie as I paced the hospital. I remembered the little girl who used to follow me everywhere and how much it annoyed me and how much I would give anything for that attachment now. I remembered when she came out to me. We were out back, raking leaves for Mom. She said she had to tell me something and I had to promise not to laugh. She told me she was into girls, and I told her I was sorry for her future heartbreaks.

On the drive back from the hospital, I drove as if Vivian had a knife to my throat again, but even after keeping an arm's reach between us while walking her to her door, when she craned her head to intrude my downward gaze, I felt like I could look into those blue eyes forever.

"Keep me posted," she said.

"I will."

Then she put her arms around my neck and pulled me in for a deep kiss that got me instantly hard. I got an overwhelming urge to punch myself in the crotch. How could I get a boner at a time like this? I tried to hide it, but she gave my cock a squeeze before knocking on the door. I walked back to my car before her mom or dad answered, and then I drove back home.

I pulled into my driveway as a cop car was pulling away. Mom was a nervous wreck when I found her pacing aimlessly in the kitchen. She became a sobbing mess when she laid eyes on me. After a long time holding her in the living room, she managed to collect herself long enough to say I should tell my dad.

"I'd do it myself, but . . . " she said, as if that was enough of an explanation.

Truth was, she didn't need to remind me of anything. No kid forgets something like his parents not being on speaking terms.

I gave her a final squeeze and went to my room to do what she wouldn't.

One ring short of the voice mail, he picked up.

"How the hell are you?"

"Not great. Jamie's missing."

"What do you mean *missing*?"

I told him what I told Mom, and for a long time, it was all silent on his end. I wondered if he was crying, too, hand over the phone so I couldn't hear.

"Dad," I said, "you there?"

He breathed deep through the phone. "Will the police want to talk to me?"

"I dunno."

"I suppose they will."

"I'll let you know if I hear anything," I said, meaning, *I'll give you a heads up if you've got shit to flush.*

"Yeah, you do that."

We disconnected and I called Greta. She didn't answer. I left a message asking her to call me back immediately.

I thought about calling Pumpkin Ghost next but couldn't do it. I was a shitty friend, a shitty brother.

I sat there in the dark for a long time, restlessly shifting until I eventually dozed off. I dreamed of Vivian's room and her shelf full of journals. I opened one after the other. Every page was empty.

The phone rang and pulled me out of the darkness.

"Greta."

"Hey. Everything okay?"

"Not really."

"What is it?"

I told her as best as I could, leaving Vivian out of it. "Kathleen is in the hospital. They found her by the tracks, covered in blood and kinda out of it. Nobody's heard from Jamie. She's missing."

"Oh my God."

"Yeah."

"I'm guessing you're not coming to the Trail tonight."

"Yeah, probably not. Can you let Kip know? I know he won't be happy."

"He'll have to get over it. Your fucking sister is missing."

I thought about asking what she had seen at the quarry the other night and if she still thought about our tryst the week before. I thought about it, but I didn't say anything.

"Hey, well, I think Ghost and I will be hanging out after. If you need a distraction or anything."

"Abiding Glory. Meier Crypt."

"We're predictable, huh?"

"Predictable isn't always bad."

"No," she said. "No, I guess not."

"Hey," we both said at the same time, then paused.

"What is it?" I asked.

"Nothing, I guess. Just . . . if you need anything . . . "

"Yeah," I said. "Yeah, I'll call."

"You have friends. We're here for you."

We're here.

Did she not know how badly I wanted her?

"I appreciate that," I said.

"Sooo, should we get an extra forty for you?"

"Yeah. Yeah, sure."

"Good. Hey, Jamie will turn up. Kathleen just probably hit her head or something."

"Or something."

"We have to hope for the best, right? Even when we feel our worst."

"Yeah. You're right."

We disconnected and I tried to sleep some more, but it turned out to be a lost cause, so I went for a walk instead.

My house was situated next to an impressive stretch of woods. Pennsylvania has a lot of impressive stretches of woods. The one by my house wasn't as thick as the one by the quarry, especially now with all the leaves dying, but it was still dense enough and private enough to wander through. It had served as the setting for so many imaginary games when I was growing up. Sometimes the trees were buildings in a futuristic city. Other times they were a haunted place, full of ghosts. Now, I was starting to feel like ghosts were everywhere and in us all. I had mine. Greta had hers. Jamie and Kathleen and Vivian. Pumpkin Ghost and Kip. Latoya. We were haunted, all of us, and the ghosts that haunted us were haunted too.

With the night to myself, I decided to go home and try making some music. I had a vocal sample from the refrain of Donovan's "Season of the Witch" I had been dying to use for something. I figured with it being October and all, now was as good a time as any. I dropped the sample into Fruity Loops Studio, distorted it a little, and gave it some delay. Then I put my headphones on and just let it play on a loop. I closed my eyes and let every note sink in. This was how I worked most of the time. I found a piece of music I liked—sometimes sampled, sometimes something I composed on keyboard—and came to know it intimately. Then the piece became a foundation upon which I could build a song outward and forward, like paving some strange road.

But it wasn't working today.

The sampled refrain, cool effects and all, failed to reveal more to me. Even though I had taken it from a song that had special meaning, a song which embodied my favorite season, filling me with wondrous excitement and dread all at once, I could not build upon it, because I was lost. The loop became an intimate and infinite haunting.

6

The Quarry, Night

went back to look for Jamie. I didn't expect I would find anything, but I had to do something. Nothing had grown from the looped Donovan sample. My friends were having the time of their lives, playing monsters at Kip Creeker's Trail. I told myself Vivian's presence had distracted me and maybe I could help Jamie best if I struck out on my own. Sure, the possibility loomed that Kathleen would come to and tell the police what really happened, but it also stood to reason that she might never wake up.

I slipped under the fence and shined the flashlight into the woods ahead. The dark between the trees whispered secrets in a language I would never know. An earthy smell hung about me. I wished I could see more, but the flashlight beam only went so far. Dead leaves and underbrush gave way under my feet. I couldn't quite bring myself to call Jamie's name. I wasn't even sure what that might accomplish. If she was dead . . . *fuck*, I really didn't want to think about that, but it was *all* I could think about. Would I find her in a shallow grave? Would it be better to not find her at all? Was closure worth terrible knowledge?

I had no answers.

I tiptoed through the darkness, resisting the urge to point my flashlight at every sound made by something other than myself. Not everything warranted investigation. Some sounds were just regular noises of the night.

All but the awful howling coming from too close behind

44

me—that was no coyote. And I was pretty sure we didn't have wolves in the area.

Pretty sure. Maybe.

I spun around, slicing at the darkness with the flashlight, but saw only trees. I crept farther into the woods, the darkness seeming more and more like this living thing that pressed upon me from all directions.

I found myself wishing I'd brought a weapon. Maybe I needed Vivian, after all. Well, her knife, anyway.

The thing out there with me howled again. I froze. I thought my bladder might explode.

I should go back.

The thought intruded. It sounded like Mom's *worried* voice. She used it whenever I didn't brake when she wanted me to on those rare occasions that I drove her somewhere. She also used it when reminding me of deadlines like school applications. Avoiding car crashes and meeting deadlines were met with the same sense of urgency. I heard this urgency now.

Run!

I wanted to listen to her. I really did. However, I had to at least try to find Jamie again. Giving up now, scary sounds in the woods or not, would make it hard for me to look at myself in the mirror in the days that followed. I walked on.

Twigs snapped and leaves rustled under every step I took. I fought the urge to wince each time it happened. Slowing my pace, no matter the direction, would undoubtedly lead to my death. Even if that howling thing didn't disembowel me, even if it posed no threat at all, spending as little time in these woods as possible seemed like a great idea. One of my brighter ones, really.

Why the fuck did I come out here at night?

I've certainly seen enough horror movies to know better.

Shit!

The wolf or whatever the fuck it was howled again. I

quickened my pace. The flashlight beam bounced like a ghost hopped up on Monster Energy. My breath rushed in and out. Running would make it hard to find anything, but I didn't care. That third howl sounded a hell of a lot closer than the previous two. I couldn't even pinpoint where it came from. Maybe still behind me, but I couldn't be sure. The awful notion that there may be more than one of those howling things out there made me run even faster.

Up ahead, the shadows shifted. I skidded to a halt. Nearly busted my ass.

Two yellow eyes opened in the darkness. White teeth gleamed in a snarl.

I couldn't tell where the shadows ended and the wolf began.

Is this thing part of the fucking shadows?

I spun on my heel. My legs tangled and I nearly lost my footing. I thrust out my arms and regained my balance.

Then I ran. I ran like I hadn't run since middle school, back when I still got out and did physical things other than sex and the occasional hike. The beast gave chase. I could hear it smashing through bramble and brush as I broke into a full sprint. Wet guttural growls came from the wolf's throat.

I had to get back to my car.

Sorry, Jamie.

I had to get to my car, drive away, and never think about the quarry and these surrounding, godforsaken woods ever again.

Impossible, yes, but I wanted to believe, desperately to believe that I could survive this night and leave this terror behind me.

Had this beast killed Jamie?

Maybe it is Jamie.

A crazy thought, but I was crazy now.

My lungs felt like they were on fire. My heart felt like it might explode.

My foot slid in a patch of mud, and I rammed face-first

into a tree. Stars splashed across my vision and next thing I knew, I was lying in a patch of dead leaves, branches and treetops spinning overhead.

The wet rasps of the wolf, its heavy footfalls drawing closer.

Then, with a gust of air, the creature passed, so close I could smell its wet dog stink.

Hint taken.

I found my flashlight, staggered to my feet, and ran back to the fence. Crawling under, I gave the wilderness one final look.

Something glowed, back near the quarry. When I got back to the car, I checked the time.

Somehow, it was already midnight.

I drove toward Abiding Glory, my heart rate decelerating. My rational side was already hard at work demystifying the beast I saw in the woods. It was a coyote, of course, just a large one. Or maybe it was a wolf that had somehow made its way into our neck of the wilderness. Nothing supernatural or strange about it. It was a brush with death, sure, but not unusual for wandering the woods alone at night. Ghostly apparitions I could accept. But werewolves?

Then there was the lost time to account for. I was not in the woods that long, yet it was now after midnight.

Was I abducted by fucking aliens or something?

I pulled over a few hundred yards from the cemetery entrance. I couldn't see my friends like this. They were just too protective of me, especially after Vivian. If they knew she was back, that I had *taken* her back, I would never hear the end of it. Now, with Jamie missing and whatever the hell happened tonight . . . God, they would probably lock me in a room for safe keeping.

Not that I would have minded getting locked up with Greta. Of course, I doubted it would be *that* kind of stay. Shit, Pumpkin Ghost would probably have me hole up at his place to prevent such a thing, especially if he already suspected something, which I was sure he did.

I put my car back in drive and headed home, flaking out on my friends for pretty much the first time ever and feeling like a total shit about it, but knowing damn well I couldn't be around them, or anyone, tonight.

I had failed in my search for Jamie (again) and was frightened by the implications of what I had experienced.

All of it—Greta's vision, Jamie's disappearance, Vivian's return, the beast in the woods—was probably a series of singular events, tangentially related at best, but because it all happened in my world, *to* me, I couldn't help but see it as one larger whole, something terrifying and cosmically significant, at which I was somehow the center. I knew it sounded crazy even then, but another inner voice, one I would never let speak out loud, told me I was a part of something big and awful, and deep down, I believed it.

Something was happening to me and the people I loved, and these past few days were only the beginning.

I drove aimlessly down dark roads which wound through wooded hills. The occasional rundown farmhouse loomed in a clearing like a misshapen gargoyle haphazardly assembled from termite-eaten lumber. I knew these roads well. I drove them a lot in the weeks after Vivian left, sometimes stopping to admire the dense scattering of stars in stretches of sky untainted by light pollution.

My phone went off a few times, probably messages from Greta and Pumpkin Ghost, but I made no move to check. I just kept driving until a mix of boredom and exhaustion sent me back home.

From the lights in the windows, I could tell Mom was awake.

Fuck.

I thought about getting back in my car and driving some more, but the last thing I needed was to pass out at the wheel and hit a tree.

Or a person.

Is that what happened to Jamie?

Haunted Hearts

No, Jamie got eaten by a werewolf, dummy.

I really needed some sleep.

I shuffled to my front door and entered. Mom had the television on, its volume nearly muted. Her phone sat in her lap, and she barely looked up from it when I entered. Her eyes were red, but it didn't seem like she had been crying. I suppose that well sometimes runs dry no matter how scared or sad you are.

"Hey," I said. "Why aren't you asleep?"

She rolled her head slowly in my direction. "You don't look well," she said. "You look pale."

"I'm okay. Just worried, too, I guess."

She pulled a cheap-looking photo album from the end table. I recognized it but was surprised she still had it. I thought she converted all our family photos to digital years ago. She opened it to a page about a third of the way into it, then held it out to me.

The spread of photos all came from Halloween a decade before. The first picture showed all of us. I was nine years old and dressed as a vampire. Black cape and slicked-back hair. Blood stains on the chest of a white dress shirt. Face painted a pale green. Was baring my plastic fangs in a snarl I thought was so scary at the time. Jamie, six, wore a red devil costume. Mom had even drawn a little black goatee on her chin. She held her tail, its arrowhead tip pointed downward. She looked so cute, gaze down and to the side. I remembered how camera shy she used to be, something she outgrew later, after learning the art of the selfie. Mom stood beside her, wearing an oversize witch's hat and a straw wig. Dad was dressed in a blood-spattered New York Yankees uniform, his eyes darkened to look bruised, an angry-red gash in his cheek.

My hands shook. I just wanted to go to sleep.

"Look at us," she said. "It feels like yesterday."

It didn't to me, but I thought saying so would be wrong. If looking at these photos had happened without Jamie disappearing, I would have probably just teased Mom about getting old. I could hardly imagine doing such a thing now. Had I grown up some? I doubted it. Up until that point, I had resisted growing up as best I could. Community college. Making music with friends. Part-time jobs. All of it made up a collective effort on my part to avoid becoming a man, an adult at all, really.

All the adults in my life regretted growing up. They never said this, but I could tell. It was in the way Mom sometimes tried to hang out with me at diners late at night or go to the movies with Jamie on weekends. It was in the way Dad ruminated on his separation from Mom, and the early, happier days of their courtship.

I thought of him now as Mom stared up at me expectantly. Awful as it is to say, I wanted what Dad said about women to be true. I wanted her to shut down her emotions or lie to me. Expecting your child, no matter their age, to be your emotional crutch felt wrong to me on some fundamental level. She was supposed to be strong for me. It was *my* turn to fall apart. I was still a goddamn kid in a lot of ways. *Her* kid, not her fucking therapist.

"I think I should go to bed," I said, handing back the photo album.

I expected her to say more, but she just gave me a wry smile and said *good night*.

I went to my room, plopped down on my bed, and checked my phone. Messages from Greta and Pumpkin Ghost.

Pumpkin Ghost: YO, PUSSY. WHERE YOU AT?!

And three from Greta:

HEY. ARE YOU COMING OUT?

DON'T LET US DRINK THESE FORTIES BY OURSELVES!

The third had come sometime later.

DUDE, WE NEED TO TALK.

I stared at the message, suddenly no longer bone-tired. My mind flooded with possibilities.

I typed a response: HEY. SORRY I DIDN'T MAKE IT OUT TONIGHT. TIRED. WHAT'S UP?

CALL ME, she typed back.

Uh oh.

I took a breath and pressed the CALL button. She answered on the first ring. She sounded wide awake. Her tone was sharp with worry.

"Hey," I said. "Sorry I didn't make it out tonight."

"Did you know Vivian was back in town?"

My gut clenched. I said nothing.

"You've seen her," she said, not even trying to make it a question.

"How did you find out?"

"All her social media is back up. Her profile pic is you and her. The one from Saint Andrew's Fair a couple summers ago."

I knew the one. It was a selfie Vivian took of us while we were upside down on the Ring of Fire.

"She's saying you two are still together."

"I need to tell you something," I said.

"Yeah, no shit."

"Look, please, Greta. This hasn't been a good couple of days for me."

"It hasn't been great for me either. And it's gonna get a hell of a lot worse for both of us if you tell me what I think you're gonna tell me."

"Why do you even care? You fuck me, behind our friend's back, ask me to pretend it never happened while you go back to him, and now you're gonna get mad at me for taking Vivian back?

"So, it's true?"

"Yes, it's true. So, what?"

"Pumpkin Ghost and that bitch are *not* guilty of the same crimes."

"You keep circling around shit he's done. What did he do to you?"

"It doesn't matter."

"It does."

"He didn't pull a fucking knife on me. That's for sure.

51

He didn't disappear without a fucking trace for a year and leave us to pick up the pieces."

"Do you think he loves you?"

"Yes."

"Do you love him?"

"Yes, and I love you, too. That's why I care, Moon Boy."

"You love me too."

"Is it that hard to see? Is it really?"

I said nothing.

"I love you," she said.

I remained silent. She sighed.

"Look, whatever. Just be fucking careful, okay? Have there been any updates on Jamie?"

"No," I said, nearly choking on the word.

"I'm sorry your sister's missing, but don't use that to justify making bad decisions."

"I'm not."

"Yeah, well. Keep me up to date," she said. "On *everything*."

We hung up, and I couldn't stop shaking. She wasn't wrong thinking Vivian was bad for me. I knew that, but what the fuck was I supposed to do? Wait around for her? Betray my friend again? Neither prospect held any appeal. Vivian wasn't perfect, but she would have to do. Ultimately, Greta would have to understand. So long as there were no knives, no sudden disappearances—

What if whoever was after her comes back?

What if he already has, and that's what happened to Jamie?

I was drawing connections that probably, *definitely*, weren't there, but dread sat like a sandbag in my gut. Tired as I was, I wouldn't be falling asleep anytime soon.

7

A **week passed with** no word on Jamie. I managed to avoid Vivian by telling her I had work and classes and band practice. I wasn't lying: I had a few shifts at the furniture warehouse and I had a music history course I was taking at the community college. Plus, Eldritch Youth did try to practice two to three nights a week, except on weeks we had live gigs. To keep her at bay, however, I had to exaggerate the workload a little. I wasn't crazy about stretching the truth, but I simply needed space after Jamie's disappearance, not to mention everything else I had on my mind. Keeping Vivian away definitely freed up some mental energy. She was easier to resist over the phone. She asked several times about coming to band practice, but I told her I wasn't ready to bring her around the others yet. Of course, this prompted her to ask if I was ashamed of her. I told her that wasn't the case, but that the others were protective of me, and I wanted to make sure the air was really clear. She didn't know about my phone call with Greta.

Kathleen was still in the hospital. I felt bad for her parents. That wasn't going to be a small insurance bill. She also had yet to speak a word. I wondered if she would be silent forever, if Jamie would be missing forever.

I spent a lot of time taking care of Mom. Mostly, I just stayed up late listening to her talk about how much she missed Jamie and how worried she was. The moments

53

where I thought she might cry were tough, but I managed to steel myself and her tears never came. I suspected she was saving them for when she knew she would need them.

Dad texted a few times.

HEAR ANYTHING?

ANY WORD?

POLICE CALL YOU BACK?

Each time, I wanted to tell him if I heard anything, he would be one of the first to know. Instead, I typed back NO, UNFORTUNATELY NOT.

I convinced myself whatever happened in the woods was a result of nerves and exhaustion, not an encounter with a werewolf or a case of alien abduction. I even worked up the will to return to those woods, eventually finding my way back to the quarry—more than once, but always at or near midnight. But every time, I waited for the house to rise and was met with disappointment when the quarry stayed dark. I looked on local social media groups and online paranormal forums for any information about the Girl on the Borderland. I saw a few accounts from people who said they'd seen her, but most of what I found was people saying there was no evidence and whatever people were seeing was some natural phenomena. I downvoted any comments from skeptics but never found the courage to argue because I didn't think it would do any good. I kept going back and looking, though. I didn't know for sure that the floating ghost house and the strange Girl inside had anything to do with my sister's disappearance, but when things were weird as they were now, it was hard not to draw connections, even when I almost convinced myself I must be reaching.

Latoya called me that Wednesday. I didn't recognize her number and almost didn't answer the call, but I thought it might be one of the detectives, so I picked up.

"It's Latoya," she said.

"Oh," I said, sitting up in bed and dropping the old issue of *Doctor Strange* I'd been reading. "How's your foot? How'd you get my number?"

"Kip gave it to me, because I wanted to thank you for taking me to the hospital. He told me what happened to your sister. I'm sorry."

"Yeah, thanks. I appreciate that."

"Do you need anything? I mean other than your sister to turn up okay."

"I don't know."

"Think you'll come back to the Trail anytime soon?"

"I hope to. Not sure yet."

"Well, I'm going to be in a boot until Thanksgiving, so I won't be able to fulfill my dream of playing final girl either."

I tried to laugh. I wanted to laugh for her. The laugh came out dry and noncommittal.

"Hey, listen," she said, "if you need to take your mind off things, maybe you want to go out Friday?"

Her proposal caught me completely off-guard. I sat up straight. My mouth moved, but no words would come.

"You there?" she asked.

"Yeah, just . . . "

"Not interested?"

"No! I'm definitely interested, just wasn't expecting you to ask, I guess."

"I'm very forward. Hope that's okay."

"It's okay."

"So . . . what do you say?"

I thought of Vivian and the conflicting emotions her return inspired. I thought of my longing for Greta and our phone call that may or may not have been a fight.

We should probably pretend this never happened.
Just be fucking careful, okay?

Latoya was someone new. She was different. She was cool and cute. She was clearly interested and didn't give off Vivian's psycho vibe. I sometimes liked to tell myself I hadn't known how unstable Vivian was, but I had always known. Her damage and danger had thrilled me from the very start.

"That sounds great," I said.

"Great," she said, then she gave me her address and all of a sudden, I had something to look forward to.

Friday night, I was being a girl about deciding what to wear. I settled on a black polo and a pair of khakis. I even put some product in my hair and put my contacts in. I had to drive back to the house twice, first having forgotten my wallet, then the red tulips I bought her that afternoon. Was I doing too much? What if this wasn't even a date? *Fuck.*

Outside her house, I had a minor moment of panic over whether or not I'd remembered to put on deodorant. I sniffed my arm pits and shrugged to myself.

I swiped the flowers and walked up to her door. She lived in a suburb called West Dale. It was a lot more developed than the wooded section where I lived with Mom and Jamie. Thinking of my still-missing sister gave me pause before I rang the doorbell. Finally, with a sigh, I pressed the button, held up the flowers and put on a smile.

A tall man with short, spiky dreads and an eyebrow ring answered the door. He was shirtless and cut to shreds and I worried I was blushing.

"Uh, hi," I said, putting as much bass into my voice as I could muster.

I held out my hand and gave him my real name.

"Mr. Johnson," he said and gave my hand a squeeze.

"Oh," I said.

Then he smiled.

"I'm just fucking with you."

I laughed too loud to seem anything other than nervous.

"Tulips, huh? Nice." He looked me up and down. "Not sure about the golf 'fit, though."

Another voice came from somewhere inside, a woman's, older though, not Latoya.

"Troy, would you let that nice boy in?" she said.

The woman came up behind Troy. She was short and

56

wore her hair in a bandana. I could see where Latoya got her smile from.

"I'm Ruthie Jean," she said, and rolled her eyes. "Sounds old-timey, I know, but those were my parents. You can come on in and have a seat. Latoya's just finishing getting ready. She must like you. She's really taking her time."

Now, I did blush. I could feel the heat rise in my cheeks and wished to God there was some way to hide it.

"Here," Ruthie Jean said. "Let me put those in some water."

She went off into the kitchen while Troy and I sat down in the living room. He had highlights from the past weekend's UFC fight playing on the television at a low volume.

"You like watching the fights?" he asked.

I felt like I should say yes, but I also thought maybe I should be honest.

"Not really," I said. "I mean, I guess I don't know. I never really have."

"You should come by sometime, have some beers. I'll get you hooked."

"Uh, yeah," I said. "That sounds fun."

I thought about telling him I wasn't twenty-one, but that never stopped me from taking alcohol from adults in the past. Pumpkin Ghost's parents were *very* generous with their beer. I guess I had never had a potential girlfriend's parent be so cordial with me before. Right off the bat, he was making jokes and offering me beer. It was strange. He and Ruthie Jean looked almost too young to be her parents, anyway.

One of the fighters on the screen caught a vicious right cross to the cheek. His knees buckled and the referee stepped in to stop the fight before he even hit the ground.

"Oh!" Troy yelled.

I laughed nervously. I had not been in a fight since elementary school, when a seventh-grader accused me of stealing shit from his locker and sucker-punched me. The two-hit combo had blackened both my eyes, bloodied my nose, and fractured my cheek, not to mention the depression it put in the wall of the boy's locker room. After that shit, I couldn't imagine hitting someone, and I did all I could to avoid getting hit, which mostly meant keeping my head down and my mouth shut whenever I was around people I didn't know.

My attention diverted from the violence on TV to Latoya as she descended the stairs. She was wearing a black boot on her good leg, a denim skirt, and a blue t-shirt. I stood and wiped my palms on my pants.

"Your date got you some flowers," Ruthie Jean said, gesturing to them. They were now in a vase on a ledge separating the kitchen from the rest of the house. "Aren't they lovely?"

"They're beautiful," she said, and her whole face brightened. "Thank you."

"You're welcome."

Troy gave me a gentle slap on the shoulder.

"Come on, man. Tell her she's beautiful, too. Act like I'm not even here."

Now, I knew I was blushing.

"Uncle Troy, you need to stop scaring away my dates."

"I'm just trying to loosen him up some. Him and his golfing clothes."

"You're just mad you're not going out tonight," she said, and took my hand.

He shrugged and gave me a smirk.

"She's not wrong," he said.

As if on cue, a baby cried somewhere nearby. Ruthie Jean told us to have a good time as she rushed toward the sound. Troy hugged Latoya and shook my hand again. Then, we were on our way. Despite all the shit of the last few days, things felt pretty good. That had me worried.

Even though I knew Latoya liked horror, I wasn't quite ready to tell her I mostly hung out in a cemetery. When she

58

asked what I usually did, I told her I hung at diners, wrote music, and rehearsed with Eldritch Youth.

"Want to get some food, then?" she asked.

"Sure."

"Got a favorite spot?"

I didn't want to take her to the West. Too many Vivian memories. Plus, what if we ran into Vivian there? That would be a total shit show. Thankfully, our county had no shortage of diners. We had the Hawkeye, Golden Sunrise, and the U.S.A. just to name a few. I suggested the latter.

"The U.S.A. is pretty dope. If the right people are working, we can get drinks."

"That'd be awesome, if I drank," she said.

"Oh."

"Don't worry. I'm not judging you or anything. It's just not my thing."

"That's cool."

"We can go there, anyway, though. I like their burgers."

"U.S.A. it is!"

The ride took us about ten minutes. We sat in a booth by the window. I had not been there in a while, and it looked like the owners had renovated the place. Lots of new seats and tabletops. Gone was all the nineteen-fifties, malt shop nostalgia. No neon pink. No chrome. No old school Coke machine. It made me sort of sad, but whatever. Gimmicks get old after a while.

Just like people.

That thought came to me in Dad's voice, soft and downbeat, even regretful.

Not me.

Latoya and I ordered coffee. She asked if I heard anything about Jamie. I told her that sadly, I had not.

"That's a shame. I'm sorry."

"You didn't do anything."

Some seconds of silence passed, and I asked her if the baby I heard back at her house was her brother or sister.

"Neither," she said. "Cousin."

"Oh, right," I said, thinking of how she addressed Troy as her uncle. I assumed Ruthie Jean was her aunt.

"Dad died in Afghanistan when I was still a little girl. Mom is around, but she works a lot. She's a nurse, like I want to be."

"Damn, I'm sorry about your dad."

"I barely remember him, to tell you the truth. My memories are more . . . I guess I remember how he made me feel more than who he was."

"Good memories?"

"Yeah." She smiled. Then she said, "Tell me about Jamie."

My thoughts went to the quarry and the floating house and the Girl on the Borderland and coyotes that might be wolves that might be werewolves.

"What?" she asked.

"Ah . . . "

"It's fine if you don't want to talk about it, just . . . if you do, you can talk to me."

I thanked her and the server came to take our order.

We spent the rest of the time at the U.S.A. talking music. She recommended some EDM and trap artists I had not heard of. I told her about some black metal and Detroit techno from the nineties, stuff you could consider classic rock if more people listened to it, I suppose.

"What are you, like, forty?" she asked with a laugh.

"You know how the Internet is. Makes everything pretty much timeless."

"I guess."

"You waste time in enough subreddits, you can get exposed to anything, for better or worse. Shit that came out twenty-thirty years ago can feel new since it's new to you."

"That makes sense. Uncle Troy got me into some hip hop from a decade or so ago. Guys like T.I., Lil Wayne. That type of shit."

"*Paper Trail* is a classic."

"Oh, so you know it? That's cool. Most of my friends

Haunted Hearts

don't know what the hell I'm talking about if I mention something from before five years ago."

"Like I said, a *lot* of time on the Internet."

We laughed at that. She stirred the straw in her drink slowly. More people shuffled into the diner. The classic rock song on the stereo changed to something slower, some dubstep throwback I didn't recognize.

"Ever go on the dark web?" she asked.

I straightened and shook my head rapidly. I remembered reading something about a true crime writer and his brother going missing a few years back and having it somehow related to the dark web.

"Fuck no. I may be crazy, but I have limits."

"You don't seem crazy to me."

We got back to music and ended up talking about Eldritch Youth. She asked me if I ever sang on any of the tracks. I had to laugh at this.

"Oh God, no. I can scream and growl, I guess, but carrying a tune? Forget it. Besides, Ghost is the genius in that department."

"What about the girl? What's her name—Greta."

"Yeah, Greta."

I believe in you, Moon Boy.

"She's great," I said.

Those perfect dimples at the base of her spine—

"Plays a mean bass, too."

Latoya and I ate our burgers and I tried not to choke, tried not to think any more of Greta. We held hands on the way back to the car. Her fingertips gently stroking my knuckles.

I opened the passenger door for her, she slid inside, and we drove back to her place. Someone was still awake because the TV was on. On the way to her door, she took my hand again and I could feel my pulse in my throat. When we reached the doorstep, she draped her arms around my neck and told me not to be so nervous, and then she pressed her lips against mine and I pulled her close and

61

she put her tongue in my mouth and I thought, this is probably what heroin feels like.

She let me put her hand up her shirt so long as I stayed outside her bra. When I moved my other hand toward her hip, she gently caught my wrist and pulled her mouth away from mine.

"You should probably go home."

"Yeah, probably," I said with a laugh.

"It's not that I don't want to," she said. "Just . . . can we wait?"

"Yeah, definitely."

"Good, because I do want to see you again, so let's take our time."

I nodded and we kissed again, though with less pressure and urgency. Then she squeezed my hand and said *good night* and I staggered back to my car.

I cooled down with an old school black metal playlist on the way home. Emperor, Satyricon, Darkthrone. Nothing was less sexy than Europeans in corpse paint shrieking about cold mountains and spooky forests. The music definitely fit the vibe for those winding, wooded roads, especially with the fog that had descended on everything. I should have slowed down, but I was nineteen and feeling good and my head was a million miles away from the thing standing in the middle of the road.

I slammed on the brakes and ragdolled in my seat as the car fishtailed to a stop in front of the beast. Its eyes shone white in the darkness, twin reflections of my headlights. Its teeth were bared in a snarl. I thought of the thing that accosted me in the woods—the thing which either came out of the shadows or was a part of the shadows themselves—but no, that's not what this was. And this thing in the road wasn't snarling, it was panting.

It was Coolio, my neighbor's husky.

That fucking dog was always getting out. I breathed a sigh of relief and gave the horn a gentle honk and Coolio jerked from his stance and skedaddled back toward his home.

Haunted Hearts

The windows were dark when I pulled up to the house, which hopefully meant Mom had gone to bed. I was in way too good a mood from my date with Latoya to be much use as a shoulder to cry on. I really didn't want to think about Jamie tonight. I needed a break from the grief and uncertainty.

Still, though, I hadn't forgotten about the things that howled in the nearby shadows. I found the house key on my key ring and pinched it tight before running up the pathway to the front door, only daring to steal a glance into the wooded darkness through the protection of the living room window. Nothing large, furry, and pissed off anywhere in sight.

A phone rang somewhere in the dark room, a familiar electronic jingle. Jamie's phone flashed blue light on the end table. Mom must have plugged it in. I grabbed it off the table. The caller ID showed weird-ass glyphs instead of numbers. I slid my thumb across the screen to answer and put the phone to my ear.

"Hello?"

Static answered back, a scrambled signal.

Then, a soft whimper.

"Jamie?"

The voice on the other end called me by my real name.

"Jamie, where are you?"

Another pulse of static replied. A second voice broke through, something impossibly low, almost sub-bass level. It spoke in a garbled, non-human language, and the call dropped. The phone was dark.

8

Home, October 17

The cop at the door kept addressing Mom as if I wasn't even there.

"It's about your daughter," he said.

He said Kathleen had woken up the night before, hysterical and rambling nonsense.

"Now, we haven't *found* Jamie," he said, "so it's possible it's not entirely true, but . . . "

"But what?" I said.

To Mom, he said, "Well, it's also not entirely clear what she remembers. Kathleen said someone was chasing them through the woods near the cornfield where your son and his friend found her. She said a train was coming just as they were coming up by the tracks. She managed to get over the tracks just before the train came by, she said, but when she looked up and the train had passed, your daughter wasn't with her."

"Are you saying my Jamie was hit by a train?" Mom asked.

"We don't know, ma'am. It sounds like Kathleen isn't too sure either."

Mom clapped one hand over her mouth and gripped my shoulder with the other. I did my best to keep her from collapsing, my own legs like wet noodles.

"But you haven't found her?" I said. "Right?"

Again, addressing Mom: "Right. And no engineers reported anyone getting hit that night. It's possible . . . "

Haunted Hearts

"I'm sick of possibilities," I said. "I want some answers."

"I understand how awful this must be, ma'am, but I assure you we're going to do . . ."

I couldn't stand it anymore. I stomped off to my room and punched a hole in the wall. The cheap material gave pretty easily, but I scraped my knuckles on the wooden frame and cried out. I cast a hateful glance toward my television and pulled it from its stand. I lifted it to smash it on the floor, but I hurled it onto my bed instead. I sat down beside it and put my face in my hands.

No crying, though.

Mom closed herself off in her room after the cops left.

I called Dad and told him what we'd heard, and the fucker laughed, not like he thought it was funny, but maybe because the news gave him a touch of hysteria. He told me he needed to go, still laughing, but starting to crack into something that sounded more like sobbing.

I needed someone to talk to. My thoughts drifted to Latoya, but I couldn't burden her with this kind of thing after one date. Nothing would scream unstable and needy like asking a new crush to help you process your familial grief.

Vivian was the last person I wanted to see, as bad as I wanted to just fuck someone and empty my head of all the noise.

And there was already enough emotional tension in the air between Greta and Pumpkin Ghost and me . . .

I felt very alone.

I closed my eyes and saw the Girl on the Borderland in the window of the floating house above the quarry. Her eyes were soft, and her lips were slightly parted. Remembering the vivid details of her face, as if only a few days had passed and not a few years, I now had somewhere to go. But it would have to wait until midnight.

I had nine hours to kill before a trip to the quarry would mean anything, and I couldn't focus well enough to work on music, so I drove to the U.S.A. and prayed whoever was working would have no problem serving me booze.

I supposed I could play the dead sister card, but I really didn't want to jinx it and ruin any hope for finding her alive. Though I didn't consider myself superstitious, erring on the side of caution probably couldn't hurt.

A spot Pumpkin Ghost would have called *rockstar parking* awaited me under ten paces from the entrance. I parked and went inside. A wave of heat made my skin feel instantly dry. This shit hole could never find a good temperature. In the summer, it was like walking into the tundra. Now, not a month into the fall, they had the heat on full blast. I peeled off my hoodie and sat at the bar.

Miles was working tonight. He was a drummer in two metal bands and one jazz combo. With his perpetual scowl and broad shoulders, he looked tough. He was your classic gentle giant though, soft-spoken and, much to Pumpkin Ghost's delight, generous with his weed. Best of all, he had no qualms about serving me alcohol. Maybe he even thought I *was* over twenty-one, not that I looked it or anything. I don't think he ever carded me.

"Just in time for happy hour," he said, putting a square napkin in front of me.

It didn't feel like happy hour. I was the only one at the bar. Miles handed me a double-sided, laminated menu.

I chose something that looked like it would be strong enough without tasting like shit.

"I'll get you a double," he said, with a wink.

He came back and put a drink with layers of red, yellow, and blue in front of me. I couldn't imagine what was in it and frankly, I didn't care. I took out the straw and helped myself to a healthy swig. When I finished, half the glass was empty. It tasted like candy, something a kid would drink.

"Can I get a water, too?" I asked, trying not to grimace.

He laughed and said, "Sure."

Haunted Hearts

When he finished pouring, I had finished my drink.

"That kinda day, huh?" he said.

"That kinda month."

"Yikes."

"Yeah."

"Wanna talk about it?"

"Right now, I just wanna drink."

"Fair enough," he said, taking my empty glass and replacing it with a full one.

By the time I started my fifth, there were more people at the bar. It was starting to get a little louder. I was ready to make some mistakes.

"I won't stop serving you," Miles said, "but I'll have to take your keys."

I nodded and handed them over. There were more and better mistakes to make and I aimed to make them.

After two or three more of those drinks I already knew would hurt in the morning, I pushed away from my stool and stumbled for the exit.

"Call a Lyft, homie," Miles said. "No walking home."

I waved without looking back. Outside, I slumped onto the hood of my car and pulled out my phone. I scrolled to Vivian's contact. My thumb shook over the phone icon. My whole hand trembled, and I thought I might drop the phone. I held it with both hands, no idea what I was going to do next. The world suddenly had a wavy texture, like everything was underwater. My stomach roiled and my mouth was dry.

Put the phone away.

This is a terrible idea.

Maybe not. Maybe we'll just talk.

I almost laughed at that thought. I knew exactly what would happen if I made this call.

But I *needed* to talk to her. We had to part ways so I could pursue something healthier with Latoya. Or find out if there was anything real between Greta and me.

Goddamn, I'm one messed up motherfucker.

67

Lucas Mangum

I did laugh at that. Self-deprecation was my favorite type of humor in those days.

The laugh came out dry and it sort of hurt. I pressed the phone icon before I finished.

During the seconds when the line rang, my surroundings returned to normal, and I felt very sober.

The line rang on and on until Vivian's recorded voice answered and said to *leave a message or whatever, I'll get back to you, maybe, if I feel like it*.

I couldn't find the words by the time the tone sounded, but I didn't want to seem shady by just hanging up, so I just stood there breathing into the phone like Michael Myers or something. Finally, I managed, "Uh, hey," and the recording cut off. The mechanical voice asked me if I wanted to re-record my message, but I hung up. Calling her was a terrible idea, anyway.

Not as bad as hailing a Lyft to her house, which, of course, was exactly what I did.

My driver was some hipster named Melville who tried to sell me weed and 'shrooms.

"Do I look like I need help getting fucked up?" I asked.

He gave me a long look in the rear view.

"Yeah, guess not." He paused as he made a turn off the main drag about a mile from the U.S.A. "So, where you going tonight, mang? A booty call or something?"

"Or something."

This is, by far, your worst idea ever.

That admonition came in Jamie's voice, and I started getting choked up. *Shit.* I did not need to be bawling my eyes out in front of some drug dealer moonlighting as a Lyft driver.

Or is he a Lyft driver moonlighting as a drug dealer?

I didn't know. I just knew I was fucked up something fierce and fixing to fuck up a lot more.

When we reached Vivian's house, I lingered in the backseat.

"Change your mind about those 'shrooms?"

68

Haunted Hearts

"Nah, man. Sorry."

"You're loss, mang."

Mang, like fucking Scarface.

"Yeah, later, Melville," I said, and got out.

My footsteps stuttered to a stop.

Vivian's door was ajar.

If I were sober, I probably would've stayed outside and maybe called the police. Drunken curiosity propelled me forward. I stood at the threshold, hand raised to push the door open. I took a breath and tried to focus as best I could, remembered how much her parents disliked me. If I was mistaken and there was *nothing* wrong, I could not justify barging in.

I knocked hard enough for the door to creak open. The front room was empty. I walked in despite every voice in my head screaming at me to stop. The room felt cold, colder than the outside for some reason.

"Help . . . " someone croaked from the kitchen.

I turned toward the sound. Vivian's father crawled, leaving a blood trail too big to be real.

"Help," he said again, drooling crimson.

Beyond him, Vivian's mother hung from the laundry room door with a large kitchen knife lodged between her breasts. Her limbs twitched. Her eyes showed no sign of life.

"Oh, God . . . *Vivian!*"

I turned to the staircase. Two shadows darkened the top, standing arm in arm. They descended with silent footfalls. A pair of impossibly strong, invisible hands clutched my ankles and held me in place as the figures descended with silent footfalls, their shapes lightening from black to gray—still in the shadows, but now emerging.

One of them held a knife. It gleamed with strange, white light from an unseen source.

I struggled against the clutching hands. Groaning and flailing, I desperately tried to break free. Every muscle in my body burned. I couldn't even fall one way or the other

Lucas Mangum

to give myself more leverage, such was the strength of these hands. I knew then I was going to die.

The figures stepped into the light, still arm-in-arm, now recognizable.

Vivian on the right, her features gray with death, grinning dirt-crusted teeth. A second smile glistened red across her throat.

The second figure wore a mask, a once-white corn sack, now yellowed from exposure to the elements. He wore faded denim overalls covered in dark stains. His arms were pale and withered. He held the knife in a relaxed grip, which did nothing to lessen the threat of its presence.

I renewed my feeble attempts to free myself from the shackling hands. I screamed for Vivian, I screamed for Greta, I screamed for my mother and father. I screamed, and reality melted around me.

At the bottom of the stairs, the man with the knife slipped his arm free from Vivian's and reached for his mask. He peeled off the corn sack to reveal his face. To reveal *my* face.

My twin raised the knife, pointing it at himself. He began cackling as he drove the knife over and over into his face, into *our* face. I could feel the pulsating fire spreading solar flares through my skull. Vivian joined in the laughter. Her dying parents, too.

70

9

Greta's Place, Later

woke later that night and vomited diabetically sweet bile onto someone's lawn. When I lifted my head from the putrid pile of puke, I didn't see Vivian's house.

I saw Greta's instead. The sky was still dark. I fumbled for my phone to check the time. It was a little after eleven. Given the dream's vividness, I thought I was out longer. Only two hours or so had passed, but a hangover was already starting to take hold. I needed more water and some headache medicine, otherwise tomorrow was really gonna hurt.

By some miracle, I got to my feet and stumbled to Greta's door like one of Romero's living dead.

Judging by how fucked up I feel, I'm probably more like one of Fulci's zombies, or one of the really messy ones. The Dead Next Door.

Thankfully, the door was shut all the way.

I should call before I knock.

That rational voice, though certainly my own, sounded like a stranger on a bad phone connection. Still, I figured I should listen. I held my thumb over the phone icon, my hands trembling. Texting probably made more sense.

HEY. U UP?

I waited and tried to take a few deep breaths. I had to see if I could breathe without puking. It proved easier than I imagined it would be, though I had to brace myself against the door frame. My phone chirped.

YEAH. IS THAT *YOU* OUTSIDE?
YEAH. CAN I COME IN?
I'LL COME OUT.
CAN YOU BRING SOME WATER?

The two minutes it took her to meet me outside felt a hell of a lot longer. I took the glass and chugged it, the cold stinging my throat. She had come out alone, but I asked about Pumpkin Ghost, anyway.

"He stayed in tonight. Said he's working on rhymes. So . . . how drunk are you?"

I set the glass next to a novelty gnome in the flower bed.

"Shit-bombed," I said. "Jamie . . . " A lump formed in my throat. I swallowed hard and said, "She might have been hit by a train."

"Oh my God." She said my name and put her arms around me. "Why didn't you call?"

My vision went underwater again. I swallowed another lump and tried to make myself sound as detached as possible.

"I didn't want to . . . complicate things."

She half-sighed, half-groaned.

"Look, whatever happened the other week . . . you're my friend first, above everything." She backed up to look me in the eyes. "I will always be a shoulder to cry on, especially for something like this. I can't even imagine what you're going through."

"Yeah. I appreciate that."

Her brow furrowed.

"Did you throw up on my lawn?"

"It's a long story."

"You can tell me, but you'll have to talk over the hose."

"That's fair."

She led me to the side of the house where her parents kept the hose. I unspooled it and aimed it at my puddle of vomit.

"Okay, ready," I said.

Haunted Hearts

Greta turned on the spigot and I sprayed the vomit until it sloshed into the gutter and toward the nearest sewer drain, then sprayed my face and the front of my shirt and washed those chunks into the sewer too. She turned off the water, I looped the hose back up, and we sat on her back deck. She went in to get me some headache medicine and more water, as well as some water for herself while I wrung out my shirt.

"You're probably still gonna feel like shit tomorrow," she said, coming back out and handing me the pills. "Not just because of the hangover, though."

"Yeah."

"How *sure* are they she's dead?"

"They're not," I said, then explained how she hadn't been found and the railroad companies had reported no local accidents recently.

"Well, that's something," she said.

"Yeah, I guess."

"Your parents okay?"

"They're a mess."

"Figured."

She took my hand and I reciprocated. Our fingers locked.

"This is nice, though," I said. "I'm glad you were home . . . "

I almost said *home alone* but didn't think that would go over well. Plus, I was pretty sure her parents were there.

"I'm glad I can be here for you."

Her features betrayed nothing. Her tone was as clinical as I'd intended mine to sound earlier.

"I guess since the police don't know anything, there aren't funeral plans."

"Right. No funeral plans."

"I hate funerals. I'd go for you, of course, but . . . "

Unable to find the words, she simply shuddered.

I laughed. "You spend half the week hanging out in a cemetery."

"I know. That's different for some reason."

"Is it?"

"I don't know. It feels different to me."

"Maybe you're right," I said.

I truly didn't know. Unless you want to count Jamie and I burying our cat in the backyard, I'd never been to a proper funeral. My only dead relative was my maternal grandfather who, in Mom's words, was an awful man I didn't need to know.

"My big brother's funeral still gives me nightmares," she said.

"Fuck, I bet. You were what? Ten?"

"Eight."

"Jesus."

"Yeah."

We were silent for a while. There was nothing more intimate than silence you could enjoy with someone else. Sure, with some people, you're silent because you don't want to talk to them. With others, those special people in your life, you can appreciate those moments when there is truly nothing to say. I felt this way with Greta often, and I felt it with her now. I thought I loved her more than anything. I was such a fucking fool.

She took her hand away and put it in her lap.

"So, what's up with Vivian?" she said. "Really."

"She came over, and she . . . we hooked up." Greta raised her eyebrows. I shrugged. "I was lonely, I guess."

"That doesn't go away when you're with someone."

I thought again about what Pumpkin Ghost might have done to make her want to fuck me a couple weeks ago. I decided not to ask her, because I liked the moment we were having.

"Anyway, she helped me look for Jamie, and that's when we found Kathleen. I haven't seen her since, though."

"Shit, I think I even remember you saying being *with* Vivian made you feel alone," she said, still stuck on the concept of loneliness.

"Did I say that? I guess I could see myself saying that."

Haunted Hearts

"You definitely did."

"You're right about her," I said, thinking about the drunken dream I had before waking up on Greta's lawn. "She's bad news."

"You need someone who will appreciate you."

"Or at least not threaten me with a knife."

"Or that. Bare minimum."

We laughed and she gave me a light tap on the arm with the back of her hand. When the laughter died down, I told her I went on a date with someone else.

"Oh? Anyone I know?" I opened my mouth to tell her, but she held up her hand. "Wait, don't tell me."

She shut her eyes and pretended to concentrate very hard. She opened her eyes and smiled.

"Latoya."

"How did . . . ?"

"We girls have powers you can't even fathom, young Moon Boy."

She took back my hand, this time wrapping it in both of hers and setting it close enough to her lap to get my blood up. I don't think she meant for it to be sexual, but because I still had feelings for her, I couldn't help but think of my hand as approaching God's Country.

"I'm really sorry about your sister," she said. "I hope they find her. *Alive*. I'm glad you want to stay away from Vivian. I just hope you will. I know she's got strange power over you. Maybe having a new love interest will help ease the transition."

"Yeah."

"I'm sorry we can't . . . "

I took my hand away and crossed my arms. My wet T-shirt clung to me like the damp, chilly embrace of a fresh corpse. I suddenly felt every definition of the word *cold*.

"Please don't," I said.

"You're right. I should . . . we should . . . right. It never happened."

Something squeezed my heart. Tears fell despite my

best efforts, and they weren't just for her. They were for even more than Jamie and Vivian. They were for something indefinable. A feeling I could only express in colors. Dark purples and pumpkin oranges and midnight blues, October colors. It was an emotion, yes, but *sadness* and *longing* and *nostalgia* didn't quite do it justice.

Greta put her arm around me, and I rested my head on her shoulder. She made shushing and cooing sounds that were almost motherly. I tried really hard not to think of them that way since we'd had sex only a little over two weeks before, but you have to call things what they are. I pressed myself against her and closed my eyes.

Something howled nearby. I lifted my head.

"Did you hear that?"

"Yeah, it's probably just . . . "

"No."

Behind her house, a creek separated her backyard from the neighbors. Trees and bushes lined the channel, obscuring the water so I could see no moon or stars reflecting from its surface, only black. Then a pair of yellow eyes appeared in the darkness.

A second set of yellow eyes joined the first. By the time a third set opened in the darkness, Greta and I were already standing, bumping each other as we backed toward the nearest door.

The sets of eyes drew closer, the bodies housing them still cloaked in shadow. It reminded me of my earlier dream, but much worse, more immediate. Though I couldn't make out the shapes, their considerable size cowed me. Soon, wolfish features emerged. All three muzzles snarled. Their growls rumbled deep in the low register, but each sounded distinct, like a death metal three-part harmony.

Behind me, Greta fumbled with the door.

"Is it locked?"

"I don't remember locking it."

The lupine things stepped farther into the moonlight.

Haunted Hearts

They walked on hind legs, broad-shouldered and hulking. Drool fell from the jaw of the one in the middle, a massive beast with scraggly, gray and white fur. Its teeth were jagged and curved. They looked like they could rip through even the toughest skin. Mine would pose no resistance.

Greta and I braced ourselves against the wall. I thought about running, but I didn't want to leave her.

They would probably catch us, anyway.

The wolf people had stopped coming. The gray and white one reared back its head and howled. The sound made every part of me shrivel. When the other two joined their leader in his bloodcurdling bellow, Greta and I screamed too. We didn't even realize we were doing it at first. The cries just poured out. When the wolf people stopped, we stopped. We trembled and waited to see what they would do next.

The wolf people began to twitch. First, the motion was barely noticeable. Then, they were flailing, grunting as their fur retracted, swallowed by their skin with a series of hisses and sucks. Bones crackled and muscles squished as their features shrank, becoming more human.

"What the fuck?" Greta said, speaking for us both.

The wolf people fell on their hands and knees, each of them now more person than beast. Greta and I exchanged glances, then looked back at the trio of shapeshifters. Soon, three naked people knelt in her backyard. The one in the middle stood. I couldn't make out his face, but I could tell he was an old man, his body saggy and liver-spotted, his genitalia dangling nearly to his knees. I instinctively looked away. His first words were not what I expected.

"Do you have any towels?" he asked.

I *recognized* his voice.

"Kip?" Greta asked, stealing my words.

"Oh," he said, recognizing us and covering his cock and balls as best he could.

The one on the left stood. She made no effort to cover herself. I recognized her, too, but I wasn't sure how. The last wolf person to rise covered her breasts with one arm and her genitals with her free hand. She was dark-haired, pale, and petite. When I saw her face, my heart lurched.

"Oh my God," I said. "*Jamie*?"

I ran to her, despite my reservations, even though I'd just seen her turn from a hulking beast into my naked sister. I threw my arms around her, hugging tightly, desperately. Overcome with emotion, I tried to find the words. She stroked the back of my neck and whispered something I couldn't hear over my own sobbing gasps for breath. My legs felt like they'd gelatinized, but I somehow kept my feet. I pulled away from Jamie, only slightly, so that I could look her in the eyes.

"How," was the only word I could manage.

Her dark gaze held me like a tractor beam. Her face was recognizable now that the wolfish qualities had retracted somewhere deep within her, but it held a maturity. She looked older to me now, more grown-up, as if she were somehow the older sibling. I looked from her to the other two, understanding but only vaguely. She'd found her wolfpack—grown and changed into something that could only fit in among their ranks.

I realized two things then: First, I knew she would never be coming home; second, I was saying her name over and over like a feverish mantra, a neurotic prayer.

Greta brought out coffee, a towel for Kip, and T-shirts for Jamie and the other woman. I collapsed into one of the patio chairs and tried not to hyperventilate.

"I guess I have some explaining to do," Kip said once everyone got settled.

"I'll say," Greta said.

"You already know quite a bit," the other woman said, staring at Greta. "At least a good deal of the beginning."

Greta darkened. I perked up, my eyes darting across

everyone's faces. I suddenly felt like the last person to get in on a powerful secret.

"What's she talking about?" I asked. "How's Jamie alive and . . . "

"All in due time," Kip said. "We'll talk first. If we miss anything, Greta and Jamie can fill in the gaps. We have time."

"Some time," the unnamed woman said. "Not a lot."

"We have tonight and there's still a few weeks until . . . "

"Halloween," Greta murmured.

We all looked at her. I was dead sober now. I didn't even need the coffee. I ignored the urge to protest more, to demand answers right away in the order I preferred to get them. I wasn't the one in control here. Any demands I made would be no more than shouts into the void. I waited for the fucking werewolves sitting on Greta's patio to elaborate.

"That's right." The unknown woman glared in Jamie's direction. "I'm still not thrilled about bringing these two into our circle."

"They can be trusted," Jamie said.

Kip nodded. "That's right."

She and Kip looked at each other. First, she scowled, then she softened. Kip nodded. She stared into the darkness. Her lips parted, but she couldn't seem to find the words. After a long, strange silence, she said, "My name is Alse and this year, on October 1, I rose from the dead."

She paused for a reaction. I couldn't speak for Greta, but nothing could surprise me by this point.

"In 1647, I was tried and executed as a witch." Okay, maybe *that* was shocking. "I was the first woman in America to suffer such a cruel fate. This was in Connecticut after an influenza epidemic killed a high number of children. I had nothing to do with *that*. I confess I did run with the wolves and other spirits of the woods in those days, but I never harmed any children. I never harmed anyone who didn't deserve it. My destiny was to protect the

79

children, protect the people." A strange smile played at the corners of her mouth. "Mostly from themselves.

"After they hanged me, the very wolves and spirits I ran with every night unearthed and restored me to life. We became known as Mothers of the Moon. Some ills can be cured by love, others can be banished by magic, but others require tooth and claw. We did a little of each."

"Not sure what good you did," Greta said. "World's still a shit hole. It probably always will be."

It sounded cynical coming from Greta's lips, but she had changed so much. Between fucking me one random afternoon and seeing something in the floating house she wouldn't tell me about, she seemed like she'd become a completely different person.

"You're a smart kid," Alse said. "Our enemies are quite formidable. When we win, it only happens incrementally. Every loss sets us back quite a bit."

"Like balance?" I asked.

"It's more like tension."

"Tug o' War," Kip said.

"Exactly."

"Sounds like a lost cause to me," Greta said.

"Not if you've seen what I've seen," Alse said. "I've walked the earth and places beyond this reality. I've died and come back more times than I care to remember. I've seen the engines of ruin at their most destructive, and I've seen the face of God." Either Greta or I made a face, because she clarified, "Not God as you understand them."

"So, what's going on now?" I asked. "Why are you here?"

"And what do you need from us?" Greta asked.

"I'm not sure it is the two of you I need, but there is strength in numbers, and time is short." She looked right at Greta. "And you know why I'm here."

Greta darkened. I huffed and stood with my fists balled. "Okay, but what does all this have to do with my sister BECOMING A FUCKING WEREWOLF?!"

Haunted Hearts

"Well, it wasn't the call I would've made," Alse said under her breath.

"Well, you weren't there," Kip said. I stared at him for more of an explanation. "The night Jamie went missing, she and her girlfriend were being chased by the same beings Alse came here to face. Her girlfriend—"

"Kathleen," Jamie interjected.

"Right, Kathleen. Well, she got across the tracks in time. Jamie here didn't."

I turned to my sister. "You *were* hit by a train?"

"No, I chickened out the moment I reached the tracks. It would never happen now, but I froze up."

"He would've killed her if I hadn't changed her," Kip said. "I took her back to Alse, and we looked after her while she went through the . . . well, it's like a violent fever when it enters your bloodstream. It takes time to adjust."

"I got the chills, too," Jamie said. "Lots of body aches. That's why Kip didn't help Kathleen. He didn't know she was out there too until I came out of it."

I sat back down and put my face in my hands. "I don't believe this."

"Well, you better if you want to be any help," Alse said.

I wasn't sure I wanted to be any help, but Greta was here, and Jamie. The last thing I wanted to do was show weakness. I put my hands in my lap, straightened my posture, and nodded once. I thought then they meant to turn us into werewolves, too. They had something else in mind.

10

Greta's Place, October 18

I asked Jamie to stay. She told me going back to normal was no longer possible.

"At least let Mom know you're okay," I said. "And what about Kathleen? She deserves to know what happened to you."

She just gave me a wry smile, then followed Alse and Kip into the woods. Greta and I stared into that darkness long after the wolf people left.

"You can stay here tonight," she said. Despite everything I had just heard and the roller coaster of emotions I experienced these past few weeks, her offer brought a spike of excitement. She must have seen something in my face because she then clarified, "On the sofa, I mean."

I forced a laugh and nodded. My excitement died just as quickly as it had arrived. She was right, of course. Sleeping with her would be wildly inappropriate, especially now when we had to hold things together more than ever.

She set me up in the family room in front of the television. I stuffed a throw pillow under my head and covered myself with an afghan blanket. She stood over me for a few beats. I couldn't read her features. She stood there a little longer before leaning down to kiss my forehead. "Good night, Moon Boy."

"Good night, Greta."

I lay there in the dark a long time. The place where she kissed me tingled until I fell asleep.

Haunted Hearts

The next morning, we made more coffee and returned to her back deck.

"I'm scared," she said.

"Should we have told them to get someone else?" I asked.

She shook her head. "I'm scared because I don't think I have a choice."

"Of course we do."

"You might. I don't."

"Why?"

"Stay here. I need to show you something."

She went back inside and returned with a leather-bound book.

"What's that?"

"Remember last night when Alse said I knew why she was here?"

I nodded. She handed the book to me, and I opened it.

The title page read: THIS JOURNAL BELONGS TO ELLA FRANKS

It was dated April 1982.

"Ella Franks," I said. "Why do I know that name?"

"Keep reading."

"*The monster of my dreams brought me here,*" I read. "*He's been my lover, my imaginary friend, an angel, and a demon, but this is no dream. This is his world. He brought me here, and now I am a ghost. And ghosts can be haunted, too. Especially if they have no one to haunt. This is the story of such a haunting. My story. The story of the Girl on the Borderland.*" Greta and I locked eyes. "*I hope it haunts you. I hope I haunt you, at least for a little while.* What is this? Where did you get it?"

"It just came in the mail one day back in the summer. No return address."

"Maybe Kip sent it? Or Alse?"

"Of the two, it was probably Kip. Alse didn't seem to like us getting looped into all this, but she did seem to know that I knew."

"And Kip sure didn't mind involving Jamie," I said.

"To protect her," Greta added. "I wonder if he saved her because she's your sister."

"I'm just glad he did, but I do wish somebody would've told me."

I paged through the journal some more but didn't read. The pages smelled like dehydrated flesh. The marks were inked in something with a brownish-red tint, like rust or blood. It got me thinking of ancient grimoires and books of the dead. If that's what this was, I wasn't sure I wanted to know.

"I finished it the day I . . . came over," Greta said.

"Oh," I said, knowing exactly which day she meant.

"I remembered what you said, about how you'd seen her once. Pumpkin Ghost can be so weird sometimes. He was so jealous that you saw her and he didn't. Even though I hadn't seen her yet, I needed to be near someone who had, someone I trusted. I needed to feel close to someone who maybe once felt what I was feeling. If only for a little while."

"I didn't see her the night we all went, though. I'm not sure why."

"Something must have changed."

"In me?"

"Maybe."

We held each other's gaze for several seconds. I thumbed the thick pages of the journal. "So, this is, like, her story?" I asked.

"Yeah."

"How does it end?"

"Not good."

"I guess that makes sense, her being trapped and all." I stared down at the open page, hardly reading it, then met Greta's gaze again. "What did you see that night at the quarry?"

"I saw her in the arms of a shadowy figure, someone with red eyes." She frowned. "What did she . . . look like when you saw her?"

Haunted Hearts

I thought back to that night. Me and Pumpkin Ghost wanting to see something scary and getting a hell of a lot more than we bargained for. I zeroed in on the face in the window of the floating house. I let its features become distinct in my mind's eye for the first time since that night. I felt squirmy all of a sudden.

"What?" she said.

"It's going to sound weird," I said.

"You really think *anything* would sound weird after last night?"

"She looked like my *mom*."

She sniffed and looked off in the distance. I couldn't read her mind, but I worried maybe I really had weirded her out by my confession. When the tear glinted in her eye, I got a terrible, helpless feeling, like nothing I could do could make anything better, like I might even wind up making things much worse.

"What did you see?" I asked, dreading her answer.

At first, she said nothing. She kept her gaze fixed at the very spot where the werewolves had climbed out of the thicket. When she turned back to me, her features had hardened.

"I saw myself," she said.

It made awful sense to me now. The Girl on the Borderland had no singular identity. She only appeared as whoever we wanted to protect. At fifteen, it was always my mother, this emotionally distant, tired soul perpetually engulfed by a shadow only Jamie and I could see. She never remarried after Dad left. I couldn't even recall her ever going on a date with anyone of any gender. She worked, she cooked, she slept—she'd become a sad machine. I'd wanted so badly to take that darkness from her, but I eventually came to realize I couldn't, which was why I saw nothing in that window the night we all went to the quarry. The only person I wanted to save—the only one I *could* save—was Greta when I caught her before she plunged over the edge and into the quarry's craggy depths.

Greta, who had seen herself in that ghostly window and nearly died for it.

I took the journal home and read. Her words came from the world beyond ours.

From inside the floating house.

The Shadow Realm.

After my boss, my sister, and a woman who claimed to be centuries-old all showed up in Greta's backyard *as fucking werewolves*, I didn't think anything could shock me. But this fucking story, man. *Ella's* story. It didn't just shock me. It shook me like a pissed-off kid shaking his father's beer. It shook me up so badly, I felt set to burst open. What really got to me about it: even as I read every intimate detail and felt a desperate need to help any way I could, I knew I'd never fully understand. This was her story, not mine. And that devastated me.

I pulled a forty of Old E out of my mini-fridge and drank while I read. The words intoxicated me more than the malt liquor. The Girl on the Borderland, this Ella, tried to rid herself of the demon who haunted her dreams, who took her on strange spiritual odysseys outside her body and showed her things which scarred her mind. She and her boyfriend Kip—the same Kip who would make several grimy horror movies, the same who would go on to run Kip Creeker's Trail of Terror—went out to the quarry around midnight. They had a banishing spell she copied down from one of her father's grimoires. They were young and dumb enough to think they could win.

The floating house rose from the pit just like it had for Pumpkin Ghost and me four years ago, just like it had a few weeks back with Greta and Jamie and Kathleen. There was no woman in the window, no Girl on the Borderland. There were only shadows.

When the door opened, something even more awful

spilled out. Something indescribable. A shapeless mass of non-colors. In the clutches of its ever-changing limbs, shadow people writhed and screamed. The banishing spell had the opposite effect. One shadowy figure stepped out. His features reminded her of Amon, but they were different somehow. This wasn't the calculating, sometimes playful demon of her youth. This was a being driven mad from too many centuries in Hell, and he pulled her into the awful house with him.

He was the brother of Amon, once good but now twisted, batshit.

Amon watched from a distance; his vengeance accomplished.

Thirty years in the Shadow Realm followed.

Though not quite Hell, it was far from Heaven, a gloomy land of shades situated on the border of Be'er Shachath, which was a dark and terrible place.

I tried to read more but the letters began to bleed, as if I'd spilled water on them. They became indecipherable puddles, pooling together to form one rust-colored spot. I stared as the entire page was taken over. I tried flipping it to the next, but it fell apart in my hand, as if it were merely the ashen remains of burnt paper. All the other pages were similarly charred, and as I turned them, they crumbled and blew away, covering my floor with what could only be ash. Eventually only the two covers remained, but they were no longer leathery and tough; instead, they rippled like living flesh. With a scream, I tossed the book's living remnants in my trashcan and hugged my knees as the receptacle bumped back and forth, the book covers and spine flapping and twitching like a dying bat until it fell still.

11

The Quarry, October 30

went back to the quarry with the other members of Eldritch Youth to do what was asked of us. Greta passed out pages from the spell we obtained from Alse. We'd spent the previous week practicing. We each had our parts down. I'd transposed the melody of the song into a pretty dope synth line that I recorded onto my phone. Greta had to play a chord progression on her dad's dusty, old acoustic guitar. Pumpkin Ghost would speak the words. We crawled under the fence a little after eleven, taking extra care with our instruments. The wolves met us at the quarry's edge. It was six minutes after eleven.

We waited until midnight. The house rose from the pit. It made no sound but still struck quite an image. Its angles and shapes all pale, its windows shadowed. Fog swirled around it, glowing pale shades of every color. Frightening black shapes moved within the cloud, things I could not, nor did I want, to fully see. The wolf people, my sister and Kip among them, stood around us like sentries. I could only imagine what they needed to protect us from. Alse had said our song would wage the spiritual war. They would handle the rest, the bloodshed.

Now here, now all of it real, I could hardly stand. My hands trembled and I worried performance wouldn't be possible.

"Let's do this," Greta said.

Pumpkin Ghost nodded in agreement.

Greta began to strum the chords. After four measures,

Haunted Hearts

I started the beat. Pumpkin Ghost's lyrics came hot on its heels. He spoke mostly in tongues. Pieces in our language occasionally broke through, scattered throughout the verses.

She saw me scream, can't let go . . . the floating house calls her, too . . . the shadows climb the walls again . . . his sharp teeth, bared for you.

More strange tongues. Something, many somethings, shook the trees behind us as they tromped out of the woods. I told myself not to look.

Follow me into the rift . . . his dark and terrible gift . . . haunted house in space . . . now you find your place . . .

. . . his sharp teeth, bared for you.

The house's walls now shone red. Fire blazed in its windows.

None of it looked real. It looked holographic. Or like film projected from a dying source onto a dirty screen.

I dared a glance behind me as the disturbance in the woods grew louder. Things with triangular, bright orange eyes and branches for limbs came out of the trees. Their heads were pumpkins. The wolves engaged them.

She saw me scream, can't let go . . . the floating house calls her, too . . . the shadows climb the walls again . . . his sharp teeth, bared for you.

Pumpkin Ghost chanted like a Pentecostal preacher, breaking familiar words with unfamiliar gibberish. He sounded possessed. I stole a look at his eyes. They glowed neon green. He *was* possessed.

Follow me into the rift . . . his dark and terrible gift . . . haunted house in space . . . now you find your place . . .

. . . his sharp teeth, bared for you.

A red crack, a deeper red than the rest of the house, split the door. Behind us, Kip, in wolf form, scuffled with two pumpkin fiends. The Alse wolf lifted a pumpkin fiend overhead and hurled it over the precipice. The Jamie wolf pinned one to the rocky ground and clawed at its pumpkin head, opening gashes that bled bright orange like lava from cracks in the earth.

Follow me into the rift . . .

. . . his sharp teeth, bared for you . . .

. . . haunted house in space . . . now you find your place . . .

. . . his dark and terrible gift . . .

I exchanged a look with Greta. Her face told a frightening tale. I knew she felt what I did: something was wrong. Very wrong.

From the red crack, a frozen image of hellish lightning, came a legion of voices guttural and shrill, full of pain and rage and raving hysteria. More pumpkin fiends spilled from the woods, overwhelming our guardians. I called to Pumpkin Ghost, using his real name. Then he grinned at me with a mouth that was no longer his. Needle teeth like those of a deep-sea fish filled it instead.

. . . his dark and terrible gift . . .

. . . sharp teeth, bared for you . . .

Greta screamed. She dropped her guitar, which was suddenly ablaze. My phone turned the color of ash, the synth and beat warped into something unfamiliar, a repetitive, tritone ear worm for the damned. The legion of voices joined it, harmonized in their dissonance. Pumpkin Ghost's feet lifted off the ground, his clothes engulfed in flames, which blackened into flowing robes.

Red light spilled from the crack as it broke the door frame and ascended to the house's peak. On its way up, it split into a two-pronged pitchfork shape.

The wolves lay behind us, subdued by pumpkin fiends. The cacophony reached an overwhelming volume. The red light washed over us all.

. . . haunted house in space . . . now you find your place . . .

I reached for Greta's hand, but could no longer see through the blinding red. I thought I heard her call to me, but her voice was one of many, snuffed by the cries and laughter of the others. I thought my head might split. When blackness enveloped me, it felt like it had.

12

October 31, A Haunted House in Space

awoke inside a coffin. I didn't know my name. Silence surrounded me. All was dark but three finger-sized holes in front of me. I wasn't lying down, nor was I quite standing. I was positioned diagonally. I could move, but it took effort. Stiffness held my limbs, torso, and head. The stuffy air made it unpleasant to breathe. Motes of dust danced in the meager light like filthy snow. The only sounds were my sharp, tense breaths and a deep, monotonous drone from somewhere outside the coffin. I didn't know where I was or why I was here, but I knew it couldn't be good.

I strained to lift my hands and pushed against the wooden door. A splinter jabbed into my right palm, and I cursed. The door hardly budged, but I heard the clink of a latch. I was locked in. Involuntary moans of dread escaped my lips. They liquefied into sobs. Not very heroic, I know, but fuck you, you weren't there.

I wondered if I would die here. Would I starve? Die of thirst? Run out of air? Would someone come to kill me?

I tried again to force the door open, using all the leverage and strength I could muster. No luck. I considered crying out for help, but I still had some dignity. Besides, I highly doubted whoever put me in this coffin would show any semblance of mercy no matter how much I begged.

Who did put me in here, anyway?

Memories didn't flood back to me like they do in the

movies. Instead, they trickled in a little at a time. First, I saw a woman in a window of a house with white, translucent walls. The wideness of her eyes and the curl of her lips told me she feared something. Like me, she was a prisoner. She was the *Girl on the Borderland*. Those four words made my body seize. Somehow, I knew she was the reason I was here.

A loud, metallic bang jolted me. A slightly quieter plink followed. The lid to the coffin yawned open.

I stepped out and into a dusty room. Though I could see somewhat well, I detected no actual light source. Cobwebs hung from the ceiling like withered vines. The walls were cinderblock and filthy with age. The floor was dirt. Up ahead, a staircase ascended into darkness. Behind me, other coffins leaned against the wall. The door to the one I staggered out of had the words *Moon Boy* carved into it.

I thought that might be my name, but that couldn't be right. That wasn't a real name. The other coffins had names carved onto them, too. *Greta Graves. Pumpkin Ghost.* My head was starting to hurt. I wanted to sit but the ground was filthy.

A skeletal hand punched through the dirt not five inches from my feet. I yelped and leapt back. Another hand reached up beside it, dirt collecting around its forearm as it stretched rotting fingers. The dirt parted for another set of dead men's hands beside me. In the two remaining coffins, people were screaming. Another set of hands dug its way out from the nearby dirt. A head joined the first set. Its eyes were sunken and dark, its flesh gray. An oozing nasal cavity glistened where its nose should have been. Only shreds remained of its lips. Worms writhed between jaundiced teeth.

The zombie rose from the dirt to reveal the exposed ribs of its mostly hollow torso. It stepped out of the ground with anorexic legs. Papery flesh hung from the bones of its limbs. The rotted state of its genitals rendered the corpse sexless. Only gray flaps of mottled skin dangled between its legs.

The zombie moaned and reached for me. I stumbled backwards and bumped into another. This one was sticky, fresher.

I pushed away and headed for the stairs, three zombies in pursuit. One of them, I thought, looked like me.

I bounded up the stairs. I reached for something to brace myself against. There was no railing, only a clay wall. My hand sunk into it. Something crawled up my forearm. I slapped at whatever it was, daring not to look, pulled my hand from the wall and ran forward.

At the head of the stairs, I stopped at the door. It had three finger-sized holes at eye level. I reached for a knob and felt none. Behind me, I was suddenly cramped. The monotonous drone had resumed, or maybe it had never stopped. I heard no more screaming, no more moaning zombies. Only my sharp, tense breaths and that drone from somewhere nearby.

I was back in the coffin again.

"Fuck. Goddamn it."

I kicked the door but lacked the space to muster much force. A scream welled up inside me.

Before I could expel it, the door ripped open, revealing the same unfinished basement, but now the zombies were already out, waiting for me. Their hands fell upon me. I tried to twist from their grasp. The droning grew louder, less monotonous. I thought maybe it was speaking. I screamed and the world fell away like so many crumbling blocks.

The drone, the undead moans and my scream synthesized into the looped sample from "Season of the Witch."

But I wasn't home. And I hadn't been dreaming since the day I tried to write that song.

I was at the quarry's edge and all alone.

The floating house was a pile of rubble at the bottom

of the pit. A dark crack had opened in the opposite cliff wall. Dust clouds danced in the air around it.

I tried to move, but everything hurt.

We'd done what we came here to do, but it no longer sat right with me. I couldn't shake the nagging feeling that we'd all been deceived.

The looped sample reverberated all around as if played from invisible speakers. Using all my strength, I pressed myself to my hands and knees. I called for Greta and Pumpkin Ghost. I called for Kip and Jamie. No one responded. No one was around. Under the repeated measures from the song, I heard no crickets, birds, or toads. It was as if the woods were empty other than me. I made myself sit up but nearly fell on my side. Holding out my arms to balance myself, I staggered to my feet, head swimming and full of music. Again, I called to my friends. Again, no one responded.

I was dreaming. That was the only explanation that made any sense.

But I could feel my feet pushing against the earth. I ached all over. This felt too real for a dream.

I looked for my phone. It lay smashed to pieces at my feet. Splintered remains of Greta's guitar also lay in a similar state.

Wake up, goddamn it. Wake up.

I pinched my eyes shut and took a series of deep breaths. When I opened them again, the world was unchanged. The loop continued. I was still very much alone.

I turned away from the quarry and reentered the woods. I stuck to the path, occasionally bracing against trees to keep from falling. The sample remained the same volume. When I reached the fence, I collapsed before worming my way under it. On the other side, I stood and fell against my car. I felt in my pockets for my keys. They weren't there, but I wasn't going back to the quarry. No fucking way. I headed down the gravel drive toward the street. Everything was dark and quiet, save for the haunting loop. I screamed, fell to my knees, and struck the pavement with my fist.

But I had to keep going.

At the very least, I had to find out what the hell happened to everyone, what the hell happened to me.

I walked until I reached the stretch of road between Abiding Glory and Kip Creeker's Trail of Terror.

The music mercifully died, but silence unmercifully took its place. Both the cemetery and Kip's Trail were dark and uninhabited. The road would take me nowhere. I had to choose: Abiding Glory or the Trail of Terror.

I headed for the Trail's entrance, my footfalls the only sounds.

Upon reaching the Trail, I froze.

Dozens of corpses hung from trees lining the Trail. All of them were in their late teens, maybe early twenties. The resemblance between them all was the most unsettling thing, though maybe the corpses didn't look *exactly* like me, right? *Right?*

Every voice in my head screamed for me to turn back. They pleaded with me to go home, but home wasn't what it used to be. They pleaded with me to forget what I'd seen, but no such thing was possible. They begged me to wake up, but I didn't think I'd ever been so lucid as I was in that moment. I was witnessing some revelation, condemnation, deliverance. Each theme inseparable from the other.

Someone covered my eyes from behind.

"Guess who," a familiar voice said.

I dipped out from behind the interlaced fingers and spun to face Vivian. She smiled, her teeth like knives, each of them like the one she once held to my throat. I stood there, every muscle in my body clenching like stretched cables. The tension was so severe that I shook. In a better world, I would've gone to Latoya that night I got drunk at the U.S.A. Maybe I wouldn't have found out Jamie was alive, but at least I wouldn't be here. In the floating ghost house. With the Girl on the Borderland. My girl: Vivian.

But this wasn't a better world. A girl like Latoya, who liked me for who I was and wanted the best for me, wouldn't hurt me like Vivian or complicate me like Greta. It sounded nice, but it wasn't home; Vivian was home, no matter how haunted our house.

I held out my hand. She stepped toward me and laced her fingers with mine. With the infinite and intimate haunting loop playing from speakers we couldn't see, we walked on into a nightmare oblivion.

Afterword

September 16, Somewhere in Central Texas

Haunted Hearts is a frightening story for anyone who has, like me, struggled with mental illness. I wrote the first draft of this coming-of-age horror novella during the spring and summer of 2020, those uncertain early months of the COVID pandemic when it became more obvious that this wasn't going to be a brief crisis. We all seemed in limbo, wondering what would happen next, and what it would mean. For me, it felt all too familiar.

This book would not have been possible if not for the efforts of Kelby Losack, who helped me sharpen the prose, and Max Booth III, who helped me sharpen the story. Lori Michelle Booth, as Max's partner in crime at Ghoulish Books, and Betty Rocksteady, for coming up with that *incredible* cover art, also deserve a ton of recognition.

Special thanks to Aron Beauregard, Daniel J. Volpe, Judith Sonnet, Kristopher Triana, Shane McKenzie, and Wrath James White—I look forward to our next retreat. Big love to my readers old and new, collaborators past and present, Jean and the kids, and my extremely kind and reliable book reviewers. While I'm sure I'd still be writing even if no one was paying attention, it sure feels nice when people are, so seriously, from the bottom of my heart, thank you.

And finally, to those crazy kids from Eldritch Youth: thank you, I love you, and I hope we meet again.

About the Author

Lucas Mangum is a Splatterpunk Award-winning author of *Snow Angels, Saint Sadist, Pandemonium* (with Ryan Harding), and *Gods of the Dark Web*. San Diego-born and Philly-raised, he now lives in Austin with his family. For more info, head to LMHorror.com.

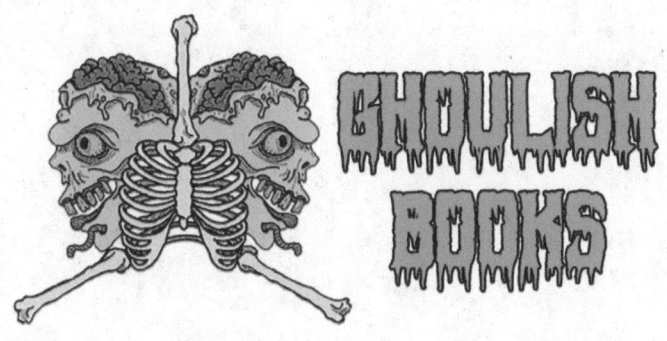

Patreon:
www.patreon.com/ghoulishbooks

Website:
www.Ghoulish.rip

Facebook:
www.facebook.com/GhoulishBooks

Twitter:
@GhoulishBooks

Instagram:
@GhoulishBookstore

Linktree:
linktr.ee/ghoulishbooks